HOMEWARD BOUND!

Corrie Returns!

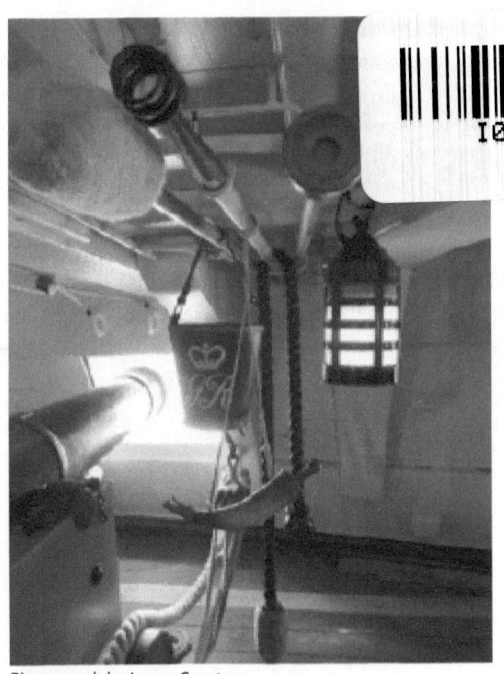

Photograph by Lance Croutear

ANTHONY BARTON

HOMEWARD BOUND! is a work of fiction. Names, characters, places
and incidents are the products of the author's imagination.
Any resemblance to actual persons alive or dead is coincidental.

BULMER PRESS ✦ ST. JOHN'S

2020 Bulmer Press Mass Market Edition
ISBN: 978-1-927721-38-4
Cover design: Nick Zelinger of NZ Graphics
On the cover: Perry's Cove, Conception Bay
Interior: Rebecca Finkel F + P Graphic Design
Copyright © Anthony Barton, 2020
All rights reserved.

PRAISE FOR
HOMEWARD BOUND!

'That the Battle of Trafalgar had given Britain command of the
sea, however many more battleships Napoleon might build, soon
became clear.'

> ... *Tom Pocock, concluding his eyewitness history of Trafalgar*

'Most of the major characters of the Nelson drama lingered upon
the stage long after his abrupt exit. He had been barely forty-seven.'

> ...*Carola Mary Anima Oman, author of the biography Nelson*

'Anthony Barton addresses one of the most serious, pervasive and
persistent sources of conflict in human experience: a conflict from
which no culture has been exempt and which probably cannot be
resolved.'

> ... *Edgar Z. Friedenberg, Professor Emeritus, Dalhousie University*

'Barton is learned in the mysteries of what it means to be human
and alive.'

> ... *Alan Milton, Emeritus Professor at the University of Ulster*

'Whoso doth the breeches wear lives a life as free as air.'

> ... *French proverb*

Corrie Has Survived the Battle of Trafalgar

It is very good of you to have bought this copy of *Corrie's War: Book 20: HOME-WARD BOUND! CORRIE RETURNS!* I should like to thank Peter Sargison, Honorary Secretary of the Chatham Dockyard Historical Society, and Tony England, Fellow of the Chatham Dockyard Historical Society, for their invaluable advice concerning the state of the Dockyard and its fortifications in the year 1806 when the battered *Victory* was brought back to that dockyard for repairs.

Corrie Harriman, the hero of my tale, has survived the Battle of Trafalgar, but it has been no easy matter for her to live through such an extensive and harrowing engagement. She is having nightmares. She has been ordered to return the *Victory* to the dockyard from which she stole that warship three years earlier. She fears the dockyard authorities may wish to settle an old score…

1

CAPTAIN SIR CORRIE HARRIMAN stood on the Quarter Deck of the *Victory* peering at Chatham Dockyard. She could barely make out the Ropery for the mist. There was no sign at all of Upnor Castle. She stamped her feet and beat her hands on her shoulders. Brrr! Despite the frigid air, she could hear the clatter and thumping that told her that the shipwrights and foundry workers were hard at work repairing the battered wrecks of His Majesty's ships after the battle off Cape Trafalgar. If she was lucky the Dockyard people would be too busy to stop her from stealing another warship with which to continue the struggle against Napoleon.

She could barely make out the dim shape of the *Fortitude* hulk and two captured vessels that had been towed to the dockyard after the engagement: the *Bahama* and the *Swiftsure*. Although the captured ships were now flying Britain's new Union flag, she felt in her bones that the war was far from over. The French would fight back. She could almost feel Napoleon's anger. She could almost feel the emperor breathing down her neck.

Over and over again she found herself reliving the worst parts of the battle. Sudden noises put her nerves on edge. She had been working hard, which seemed to help, but her dreams were troubled. She would dream of shouting to warn her father and then wake with a start, sweating. Her lover and fellow officer Tom Potts was faring no better. Poor Tom was seeing the ghosts of those he had killed. He had recounted his horrors to her in nighttime whispers.

After the battle had ended, the bodies of the dead had been piled up in heaps on the decks. Corrie herself had brought Nelson's body home to England, preserved inside a cask filled with brandy mixed with camphor. She had seen Nelson's remains buried in a ceremony at St. Paul's Cathedral in the City of London on the 9th of January. She had known and worked with Nelson, first at Copenhagen and later at Trafalgar. She was sure that Nelson would have been pleased about being buried at St. Paul's. She had overheard Nelson beg his friend Captain Hardy not to bury him at sea, and she had heard Hardy promise to bring Nelson home to England. Sadly, Corrie had seen no sign of Mrs. Nelson, nor of Nelson's mistress Emma, at that service. After the funeral, Corrie had questioned the authorities regarding the settlement with regard to Emma Hamilton and Nelson's daughter Horatia, but all her inquiries had been met by blank stares, and Corrie had shivered. Apparently both mother and child were to be abandoned and left to fend for themselves. Corrie had been moved to silent anger. Nelson's dying wish had been ignored by the feckless Prince of Wales. But what could Corrie do for Emma? Nothing. A few members of parliament would be women in the guise of men, but she doubted there were enough women in the House to pull the political strings needed to provide funds to help Emma and the little girl she and Nelson had conceived together.

Corrie was angry about that.

But there was nothing she could do.

She had to keep busy. She had to fight her demons. More important, she had to fight the French Navy. *That* was her responsibility as a naval officer.

According to her dear friend and sender of secret messages, Anne Keeper, their present First Lord of the Admiralty, Baron Barham, had ordered the Navy to *stop blockading the remains of French fleet in their naval port of Brest.*

Why?

Was Barham out of his mind?

Her thoughts crystallized.

I must be brave. I must continue Nelson's tradition, and act boldly. I shall not hang about awaiting further orders. In all likelihood, there will be no new orders forthcoming for me, now that the Admiralty has learned that I am a woman dressed as a man. Besides, a change of government is coming. So I had better seize another warship. Here I am in in command of the Victory, the most powerful ship in the fleet. Who can stop me from sailing away in any ship I fancy from these vessels I see moored here in Chatham Harbour?

Through her glass she examined the ships of war in Commission and in Ordinary laying at their moorings in the Medway. Where oh where was her own frigate, the *Swift*? The *Swift* would be her first choice. She had left her dear frigate here with her sailing master Mr. Weevil on anchor watch. But that had been three years ago. Was her *Swift* still here?

Aha! Her eye lighted on a familiar arrangement of spars and rigging. Yes, here was her frigate, moored just where Corrie had left her. But how *small* she looked after the spacious *Victory*!

Small or not, I had better grab her. The Victory *is no good to me in her present condition, being in need of extensive repairs.*

2

CHAPTER

CORRIE'S FRIEND Mrs. Anne Keeper came out on deck to keep Corrie company. 'So they didn't break her up,' she said, leaning on her stick and breathing heavily. A poisoned enemy pigeon had nearly killed Anne, but she was strong-willed and seemed to be recovering.

'I need a ship,' replied Corrie. 'We need a ship. It is good to see you back on your feet, Anne.'

'Thank you, captain.'

Corrie turned to her Danish steersman Jensen who had the wheel.

'Bring us alongside the *Swift*, Jensen. Allow for the turn of the tide.'

'Aye aye, cap'n.'

She sang out to her Officer of the Watch, who happened to be Anne's son Fraser. 'Mr. Keeper, make ready to anchor.'

'Make ready to anchor,' repeated the young officer, who had been hideously deformed during the battle. She watched him shout out a string of orders regarding the cable, the capstan, and the taking in of sail. She sensed that Fraser was not yet quite sure of himself, and needed something to challenge him. She would have to find some way to entrust him with a grave responsibility. She made a silent vow to dream up a task worthy of him, some significant undertaking that would help restore his self-respect.

The *Victory* slowed.

'Let go!'

Corrie's thoughts raced.

If I am very lucky, then the roar of the cable passing though the hawse hole will be drowned by the din of the dockyard. I had better act fast if I am to undo the mistake the First Lord has just made by lifting the blockade of the French naval port of Brest.

Tom Potts, her lover and first lieutenant, was in the forepeak engaged in a fierce argument with his new friend William Allen, that charming chemist from Guy's Hospital. They were arguing about carbon. Corrie was not sure what carbon was. She had heard that someone had just patented something called *carbon paper*. Perhaps carbon paper would be useful for firing guns?

The pair of natural philosophers beckoned to her to join them in their earnest conversation.

Corrie sighed. She was anxious to get this dockyard business over with as quickly as possible, but William Allen was her guest, and she had no wish to be rude to him.

'Yes?' she asked, joining the pair.

Tom lowered his voice. 'William has just been elected to the Committee for the Abolition of the Slave Trade. He tells me that Lord Barham knows Chatham well. He says Barham lives only twelve miles from here at Barham Court in Teston, and that Barham's wife Margaret is friends with William Wilberforce, who as you know represents the constituency of Yorkshire. Wilberforce is deeply concerned about the cruel treatment of slaves in our Jamaican plantations. My friend William here would like to have word with our Billy Brown about that. I think you told me that Billy escaped from a Jamaican plantation as a child and joined the Navy? I thought I had better ask your permission. There are political implications.'

Corrie nodded. 'There are indeed political implications. Yes, Billy has told me horrendous tales of her upbringing as a slave. I'm glad to give you permission to talk to our Captain of the Maintop, Mr. Allen. I believe the treatment of our workers in the British plantation in the Carib Sea is a disgrace. So by all means go ahead and speak with Billy, but, Mr. Allen, please talk with Billy up in the heights where you will not be overhead. If you remove your wideawake hat before making the climb, then Tom can keep the hat safe for you until you return to the deck. You will find it pretty windy up there. Are you brave enough to make the ascent? Have you every climbed up into the rigging of a First-Rate before, Mr. Allen?'

Allen shook his head. He looked up into the rigging. He was no sailor. The mast was two hundred feet high. 'If I had a boy to assist me?' her guest suggested wisely.

'Of course,' replied Corrie, and beckoned to the Spanish youth who had befriended her late father on the island of Cabrera. 'Ramón, conduct Mr. Allen to the maintop, and introduce him to Billy Brown. Tell Billy from me that she is to take Mr. Allen up to the crow's nest so they can have a private chat up there *without being overheard*. You yourself are *not* to go up to the masthead with them, Ramón. Do I make myself quite clear?'

'Sí, *mi capitána.*'

'Very well. This is Ramón, Mr. Allen. He will assist you.'

Corrie watched Mr. Allen and Ramón make their way carefully up the standing rigging hand over hand.

While they were busy doing that, Corrie took the opportunity to have a quiet word with Tom. 'Dear heart, we have to leave in a hurry. Your Quaker friend may not have a chance to go ashore.'

Tom put his head to one side and looked thoughtful. 'It may not matter to William. He is a natural philosopher like myself. After talking with Billy I think he will feel duty bound to see the slave plantations with his own eyes. I dare say he will wish to make scholarly notes concerning the conditions in the cane fields. You do recall that Mr. Allen works at Guy's hospital? Do you think he might be willing to serve as ship's surgeon? You know that we have had no doctor in our company since James Barry left to study with the Barber Surgeons in Edinburgh.'

'Good idea, Tom. Ask him. If we are going to fight the French we shall need the services of a surgeon. I cannot promise that we shall voyage as far as the sugar plantations in the Carib Sea, but you never know, we may do just that. Right now I am going aboard the *Swift* to discover what shape she's in. I'll let you know what I discover. You have the deck.'

Corrie was piped on board her old frigate by a single side boy with a whistle.

'Welcome back, captain.'

'Mr. Weevil! Good to see you again!' Weevil was a hopeless navigator, and a sentimental fool, but Corrie was fond of him.

Weevil wrung her hand enthusiastically. 'Congratulations on your victory at Trafalgar, Sir Corrie. The whole town is talking about it. What a success!'

She stared him in the eye. 'Trafalgar was an unmitigated disaster, Mr. Weevil. We lost Nelson, and I lost my father. Dad went aboard an enemy ship as prize-master, and I never saw him again. So many of people are missing. So many are dead. So very many.'

Mr. Weevil's eyes filled with tears. He squeezed her hand. 'Lieutenant Archibald Harriman was a fine, funny man. I'll miss him. We shall all miss him, captain.'

Corrie took a deep breath, She had had quite enough of the sentimental Mr. Weevil. 'How soon can we sail?' she asked curtly.

'Three months water, four months beef and pork in casks, and all expenses paid by the dockyard. We could sail today.'

Corrie's eyes narrowed. Today sounded like a *very* good idea. 'Get the crew aboard, Weevil. Fast. I want them all transferred before the Dockyard finds out I am here.'

'Aye aye, sir.'

3

CHAPTER

HER PEOPLE ran lightly across a narrow plank joining the larger vessel to the smaller. Each child, woman and man carried a ditty bag containing personal belongings. Several carried in addition certain tools vital to their trade.

Able-Seaman Kelly cradled in his arms a model ship, the result of many hours of painstaking work on make-and-mend Sundays. He made a joke about the diminutive size of the frigate *Swift* that was to be their new home. Corrie did not blame him. After the roomy *Victory*, any other ship in the fleet was going to feel cramped. To say the least.

Billy Brown ran lightly over the plank, with Mr. Allen hot on her heels plying her with further questions about the Jamaican plantation where Billy had grown up, without the slightest regard for who might be listening. Corrie sighed. Billy was explaining patiently that she was but one of several Carib Sea Islanders who had joined the crew of the *Swift*.

'Inna di morrows, *Victory*!' Billy sang out gaily, giving the greatest ship in the navy a parting salute.

Harbottle, Corrie's ancient steward, needed a bit of help from his messmates to cross the plank. He had been rendered lame by a wound taken during the battle. 'It's just me leg,' he muttered over and over again, for he was embarrassed by all the fuss.

Then the ship's carpenter dashed across, carrying his chisels in a pouch and several wicked looking tools dangling from his belt. Mr. Baird was a dependable fellow. She heard him say 'I hope she's not been left to rot,' as he looked over his old frigate the *Swift* with a suspicious eye

'Make an inspection for me, Mr. Baird,' Corrie ordered. 'Do it quickly.'

Mr. Baird nodded to show he understood her order, and her need for haste.

Norah, the ship's cook, clasping her two youngsters to her copious bosom, hastened from one vessel to the other. Though a capable soul, the battle had left her shaken. You could see the pain in her eyes. 'We're flitting,' she said to her little ones, whatever that meant. She was from Edinburgh.

Next to cross was Mark Jater, her competent Yeoman of the Sheets. He, too, hurried from one ship to the other. He was carrying under his arm a portmanteau containing his huge sail-making needles and also, swinging in his free hand, a heavy bag of brass grommets. He said not a word. Jater was no chatterbox.

Perowne, Corrie's indefatigable Yeoman of Powder, was across the plank before you could say 'Jack Robinson.' Corrie spotted the yeoman's felt slippers protruding from his pocket.

Hard on his heels came the broad-chested Sergeant Deering, sporting his best bright scarlet jacket, with his fellow Marines thumping along behind him. 'Eyes right! Salute the captain!'

John Eaves was the last to cross, carrying his long line and his log for assessing the ship's speed through the water. 'She'll be free of barnacles this far up the river,' she heard him say to himself.

'You'll have a chance to cast your log very soon, Mr. Eaves. Be prepared!' said Corrie.

Now that all of her old crew had boarded the smaller vessel, Corrie gave her officers half an hour to assign quarters and show the newcomers where to go.

She then invited her officers to her Great Cabin for an emergency conference.

Lieutenant Tom Potts was the first to arrive, being Corrie's lover and the father of her child Nathaniel, who could be heard running madly about the deck chattering to himself.

Corrie, listening to the patter of her son's bare feet overhead, deduced that Nathaniel was determined not to miss a thing. He was growing taller every day. She was proud of him. Corrie had given birth to Nathaniel while standing erect. She had been damned if she would waste her time lying down to have a baby while in charge of a warship. Besides, there had been a battle going on.

Mr. Baird, who had dashed below to inspect the timbers, reported back. He put his hand to the brim of his cap.

'Well, Mr. Baird? What do you think? Is she seaworthy?'

'She is, captain. She'll do.'

'Thank God!'

Corrie was relieved.

She clapped Mr. |Baird on his shoulder.

Arriving a trifle late for the meeting in her cabin was Mr. Tony Hartnell, the ship's purser, who had but recently returned from the Lake District. *'My apprehensions come in crowds,'* he said, and looked at Corrie questioningly.

'Welcome back to our ship's company, Mr. Hartnell. How was your leave? How did you fare with Dorothy?'

The Purser's eyes lit up. 'She and I visited the woods beyond Gowbarrow Park. We saw daffodils bursting out among mossy stones. Their bright yellow trumpets reeled and danced in the breeze. It was the happiest day of my life, captain. A host of golden daffodils!'

'I'm glad for you both. One of these days I should like to meet your poet and his sister.'

'You shall, captain. I have completed the new muster roll for the *Swift*.'

'Thank you.'

Last to join the conference was the most recent addition to her officers, the hesitant Lieutenant Partridge, carrying a telescope tucked under his arm. Partridge had been keeping an eye on the river traffic. In a ship of war, someone had to be constantly on the alert, day and night.

Now that all of her lieutenants were present, they were looking expectantly at her, awaiting revelations.

'*I dread the rustling of the grass, the very shadow of the clouds,*' murmured the Purser under his breath.

Corrie had a few dreads of her own. She had stolen the *Victory* from this very dockyard three years ago. Today she had returned the *Victory* with her mizzen mast and rigging shot through. Rough repairs made to the *Victory* in Portsmouth had barely sufficed to see the warship safely back here to the shipwrights who had labored for so many years to rebuild her at Nelson's request. In her present battered condition, the *Victory* was of no use to the Navy or to Corrie.

'We'll call the roll later. This is a meeting of senior officers. I am going to tell you what I have in mind.'

Her Great Cabin in the *Swift* seemed small and dark, especially when crowded with her fellow officers. She glanced at her new surgeon, William Allen. Looking at Allen, Corrie recalled visiting Nelson down in the darkness of the Orlop Deck of the *Victory*. There had been nothing that any surgeon had been able to do to save Nelson's life, for Nelson's spine had been shot through. The great man had lost all feeling in his legs. Surgeons were for the most part useless, if the truth be told, but having a surgeon on board was a comfort to her women and men. For that reason she was glad to have William Allen along for the voyage, even if Allen's real interest lay in discovering the truth about the slavery in the extremely profitable British sugar plantations abroad.

She thrust her memory of Nelson firmly to the back of her mind and cleared her throat.

Her mother, Admiral Wentworth, presently in charge of operations at the Naval Base in St. John's, Newfoundland, had taught Corrie to keep a wooden face. This was definitely time for a wooden face. It would not do for these brave officers here assembled in her Great Cabin to glimpse for one moment the daring, reckless plan that was forming in her mind.

The British blockade of Brest has ceased. The French will send out a large and powerful squadron to retake the Atlantic Ocean. Those in command of that squadron will have orders to bring British trade to a halt. I have to find that French squadron, or Nelson will have died for nothing. In my considered opinion, Lord Barham should be hung, drawn and quartered for lifting the blockade. But Lord Barham may know something I don't know. He is the First

Lord of the Admiralty, after all. There may be method in his madness. I hope so.

Corrie steepled her fingers. 'I have invited Anne Keeper to join us because she is expecting at an important message which may bear on what we do next, gentleman. Anne, is that your pigeon I hear?'

Anne nodded and gave her come-to-me call.

A homing pigeon fluttered in through the starboard gun port and landed on the deck at Anne's feet.

'Thank you, Mopsus,' said Anne gently, placing her left hand over the bird's folded wings while her right hand removed a slip of parchment attached to the bird's leg. She had names for all her pigeons. Mopsus was named after the Ancient Greek seer who had founded many cities. Mopsus had just delivered a long expected report from Anne's secret agent at the Admiralty.

Anne read the message silently.

She lifted her eyebrows.

She reread the message, mouthing the words in silence.

She raised her eyebrows.

'Well, what news?' prompted Corrie.

'Napoleon has sent out into the Atlantic a powerful squadron under Admiral Leisségues. The by-boats have left early for Newfoundland, accompanied by the frigate *Belle Poule*, with your brother James in command.'

Corrie narrowed her eyes. Her brother was a rash hothead. This was his first command. He would get himself and his crew killed. She frowned. 'How are we for shot, Mr. Weevil?'

'Two tiers full, cap'n.'

'Powder?'

He shook his head. 'We need more.'

'Why was I not told earlier? Have the *Swift*'s magazine restocked with powder from the Victory's Grand Magazine. See to that right away, Mr. Weevil. Do not waste a moment.'

Mr. Weevil ran out if the cabin.

They heard him bellowing 'Douse the galley! Powder monkeys to the forecastle!'

Corrie introduced their new surgeon.

'Allow me to introduce my friend, Mr. William Allen, of Guy's Hospital. Mr. Allen has volunteered to be our Surgeon on this voyage. Welcome aboard, Mr. Allen.'

The officers clapped politely. The Purser cast his eyes to heaven in silent reproach. He would have to re-write his muster.

'Have you anything you wish to say, Mr. Allen?'

'I am a member of the Physical Society,' Allen said quietly. 'I intend to bore you all to tears with my talk of carbon.'

Tom Potts asked. 'Is it true that you refuse to eat sugar, Mr. Allen?'

'Yes, that is true. I do not each sugar.'

Her officers looked at one another in puzzlement, and then at Mr. Allen, and then back at Corrie. What had sugar to do with anything?

Mr. Hartnell cleared his throat. '*Thou Eye among the blind, that, deaf and silent, read'st the eternal deep.*'

'Another verse from your friend in the Lake District?'

'Yes.'

'Anne, what else do your spy have to tell us?'

Anne glanced back at the message. 'Napoleon threw a fit when he heard about Trafalgar, and then, when we withdrew our blockade of Brest, he ordered this powerful naval squadron out into the Atlantic. My people are presently trying to find the exact composition of that squadron.'

'That will be helpful.' Corrie took a deep breath and said 'Gentleman, we must destroy that French squadron. We must act right now of our own initiative, without waiting for orders which may never come. My plan is daring. My plan may cost you your careers. My first step will be to steal this old ship of mine, the *Swift*, and sail her out into the Strait of Dover. If any of you would rather go ashore right now, then you are free to leave, and I shall write orders for you recommending you for further service.'

Her officers exchanged glances.

Corrie waited, her thoughts racing.

Will they desert me? Or will they go along with my risky venture?

Tony Hartnell, her Purser, gave her a wink. 'We are all with you, captain,' he said confidently.

'Then you all must be quite mad.'

'C-can you tell us more about the p-plan?' begged Mr. Partridge.

Corrie took a deep breath. 'My plan is simple. We shall to find the French squadron and attack it *upwind*.'

'Upwind? That's impossible!' protested her newest officer.

'I'm counting on the French to *think* it impossible, Mr. Partridge. Nelson once told me that no captain can do very wrong if he places his ship alongside that of his enemy. I plan to do just that, but it will be risky.'

'We are with you, captain,' said Sergeant Deering, speaking for his ship's Marines.

'Captain? If I m-may?'

'Yes, Mr. Partridge?'

'I hear Billy Brown singing out from the maintop. A boat is approaching from the dockyard.' Partridge bent down and used his telescope to peer out through the port. 'Here comes the new Dockyard Commissioner, Captain Harmood! I'd know that face anywhere. I served with Harmood in the *Ardent*. In fact, it was Harmood who recommended me for p-promotion.'

Corrie stiffened. The Commissioner! She was done for! Her plan to defeat Admiral Leisségues was in ruins before they had even got under weigh. 'Everybody back up on deck! As quick as you can! Go about your business! Not a word to anyone about my plan to steal this ship! Everybody out of my cabin! I had better put on my best coat to greet the Commissioner.'

4

CHAPTER

HARMOOD CAME ABOARD the *Swift* with his hand to his hat brim.

'Captain Harriman?'

'Commissioner Harmood,' said Corrie, returning the salute. 'May I invite you to my cabin for a glass of port?'

She led the Commissioner below.

She closed the cabin door to afford them privacy.

She poured glasses for them both.

'Am I to understand that you are shifting your command to the *Swift*?' said Harmood, coming straight to the point. 'I have been told that during your last visit to this dockyard you *stole* the *Victory* from us.'

'Not exactly, Commissioner. I *obeyed orders* to steal the *Victory* from the Dockyard. Nelson asked for her, you see, and he wanted her in a hurry. I do hope you know that I acted with the consent of the First Lord?'

'St. Vincent is no longer First Lord. These days we answer to Barham.'

'The Evangelical.'

'You are well informed, captain. Did you also know that Barham is making a controversial effort to abolish slavery here in England? I am told you had as a member of your crew none other than the rebel slave Toussaint Louverture? Forgive me if I find that a trifle suspicious.'

'He was the leader of a slave rebellion. Whatever happened to that fellow? I lost track of him.'

'Toussaint Louverture died in prison.'

'I'm sorry to hear that. He was a brave Islander.'

'Well, we can't have you dying in prison, Captain Harriman. But should you decide to defy our guns I have to tell you that I have forty prisoners from the American war presently housed in the prison hulk *Fortitude* moored not far from here in the Gillingham Reach. My prisoners are at work restoring the Cockham Wood fort. They have remounted an old iron forty-two pounder abandoned fifty years ago. My prisoners built a platform of tarred planks. They have remounted the weapon. My people have access to a supply of powder and shot.'

Corrie chose her words carefully. 'I think your prisoners would be unwise to try to fire their old canon at me. Commissioner, did you get that galley built? You recall that I promised to pay for the galley out of my own pocket? The East India Company rewarded me generously for bringing in the China Fleet.' She moved closer to Harmood and lowered her voice. 'I have to be able to strike the French squadron *upwind or in a dead calm.* I need that galley.'

Harmood gave her a long, hard look. 'Are you sure you have room on the *Swift*'s deck to stow your galley, captain? I have to warn you, she is *forty feet long.*'

Corrie's face lit up. 'You have built her!'

The Commissioner grinned. 'I let our fellow shipwrights at Deal build her, but I think you will approve. The Deal galleys are the best, you know. They are long, narrow and clinker built. The Deal shipwrights delivered your galley to the Dockyard yesterday. You specified elm planking and ash frames?'

Corrie dropped her guard. 'You are going to let me go and fight Napoleon,' she said, scarcely able to believe what she was hearing from the Commissioner's own lips.

'Shall we go look at your galley?' the Commissioner replied.

'I can't wait to see her. How many oars?

'Eighteen. Double-banked. As you specified.'

Corrie's eyes gleamed.

She flung open her cabin door.

'Mr. Weevil! I'm going ashore with the Commissioner. Mr. Keeper, the launch and two dozen of our best rowers. Quick as maybe!' She turned back to the Commissioner and whispered 'How much do I owe you?'

'Eight hundred pounds. That's a fair price. £20 a ton is the going rate.'

CHAPTER

The galley turned out to be worth every penny of eight hundred pounds. Gleaming with new varnish, she lay supported on balks, her keel uppermost. Eighteen oars were stacked against a wall with eighteen matching rowlocks, a tiller, a bailer, a rudder, a fluke anchor, an anchor cable and a painter.

Corrie lay on her back to peer up at the interior of the galley, and whistled. 'Leisségues is in for a surprise.' She scrambled back to her feet and brushed the shipyard dust from her uniform jacket. 'How long will it take your dockyard to put the *Victory* back together?'

'At best she'll be a second-rate. We have a timber in the mast pond that has been soaking for three years, and should suffice to replace the *Victory*'s damaged mast. Eighteen months at least, to answer your question. I do thank you for bringing our *Victory* back.' He lowered his voice. 'To answer your *unspoken* question, I cannot give you permission to steal the *Swift*, Captain Harriman, for that would surely cost me my career. The moment you set sail, I shall be duty bound to sound the alarm. Our fort at Gillingham is designed to rake the Gillingham Reach, but luckily for you the gunners will be hampered at present by several vessels moored in the line of fire, among them the hulk *Fortitude* in which I confine my American prisoners.'

Corrie absorbed the Commissioner's veiled advice. She exhaled. 'I dare not wait until dusk. I shall have to navigate the shoals at the river mouth, and the tide is turning. I shall sail soon, Commissioner. I'm sorry to leave in such a hurry. I have enjoyed our talk very much and I hope not to get you into too much trouble.'

Corrie and the Commissioner looked long and hard at one another. They were both naval officers. Both knew the importance of making an *immediate* counter to Napoleon's response to Trafalgar. The French squadron commanded by Leisségues had to be found quickly and it had to be soundly smashed in order to confirm Britain's command of the seas.

The Commissioner lowered his voice. 'I'll do this much for you. I'll delay informing the people at Gillingham for as long as I dare,' he said. 'But I have to warn you, Harriman, the moment you make sail and begin to move downriver, I shall raise a warning flag at the Dockyard and fire a warning gun. I shall then order a messenger to ride hell-for-leather to Cockham Wood with orders from me telling my prisoners and their guards to open fire on you.'

'Thanks for the heads-up, Commissioner.' The messenger would have to work his poor steed into a lather, cross the river by the Rochester Bridge, and with luck might arrive too late at the Cockham Wood Fort to prevent the *Swift* from leaving. She understood that the Commissioner had to be able to report to the Admiralty that he had made every effort to prevent the stolen *Swift* from leaving. Harmood might be retired on half-pay. Navy politics! Corrie knew all about Navy politics. She herself had faced court-martial, been pardoned, and later knighted for services to the Crown. Navy politics were old hat to her.

She and the Commissioner shook hands.

She and the Commissioner visited the office of the Dockyard Paymaster, where Corrie settled for her purchase of the galley. Eight hundred pounds was a huge sum! She had never spent so much money in her life. She took a deep breath before signing the note to draw on her funds lodged with her banker Child & Company.

Then she hastened to the riverside and ordered her people to slide the shiny new galley down the hard and into the water. Her best rowers leaped to take their places at the oars while she herself took her place on the tiny coxswain's seat in the galley's long, narrow stern.

This was the start of a fresh adventure. She could feel it in her bones.

'Give way! Put your backs into it! Let's see what our new galley can do!'

6

CHAPTER

CORRIE WAS ROWED back to the *Swift* as fast as her eighteen oarsman could drive the long narrow craft through the water, which turned out to be very fast indeed.

Just as well! She was in a hurry.

Napoleon wanted revenge for Trafalgar? Leisségues's squadron had sailed? Her brother was in danger? Corrie gripped the sides of her brand new galley.

'Lose not an hour!' had been Nelson's maxim.

The tide was on the ebb.

So it was now or never.

If only I had Nelson's talent for seeing what was coming…

She leaped from her new galley and scrambled up the side of the *Swift*.

She was piped aboard. None of her officers had deserted her. Thank God for that! All stood there awaiting her orders. Why they trusted her, she could not fathom.

'Cease transferring powder! Hoist our galley aboard. Find somewhere to stow her. Man the capstan! Action stations! Take the children below! We are about to be fired upon by the Dockyard!'

There was just enough space on the Gun Deck to stow the galley. She had calculated correctly.

The Dockyard Commissioner would have a glass trained on her.

'Hands up! Set sail!'

The moment the Swift began to move, a signal flag ran up the Dockyard masthead, and the sharp bark of a warning gun echoed across the river to alert the forts defending the Dockyard.

Immediately the air shook with the deep bark of a colossal piece from Upnor Castle.

Something very dangerous indeed came whining through the air over their heads.

'Sounds like a forty-two pounder,' said Tom Potts, mopping his forehead and looking askance at Corrie. 'I'll wager nobody has fired that gun in years. I dare say it fires a stone ball.'

Corrie dug her nails into her palm. 'They'll hear that bang at Cockham Wood. They'll know we are coming. The Commissioner's American prisoners-of-war will be loading that gun of theirs.'

The Swift caught the wind her sails and heeled, sending copper pots clattering in the galley.

'I see the fort at Cockham Wood now,' said Tom, focusing his bring-them-near. 'I see a fellow dressed in prison clothes standing on the parapet with his arm raised.'

'Steer as near to the South Bank as you think safe, Mr. Jensen.'

'Aye aye, cap'n.'

'The officer is lowering his arm!'

A great bellow echoed around the Downs. A column of white water shot up out of the river in the *Swift*'s wake. Rooks in their hundreds took to the skies cawing in alarm.

'A miss, captain. The prisoners-of-war are reloading.'

'Use the ships lying in Ordinary as cover. Keep us between them and the fort.'

'Captain! I spy Folly Point in the distance!'

'Thank you, Mr. Potts.'

'I smell the sea,' squeaked twelve-year-old Gloag, who was too old to be shut up down below with the babies. He sounded excited.

Corrie looked up and saw the boy hanging halfway up the rigging with his friend Ramón. 'Why are our own people firing at us?' she heard him ask his friend, puzzled.

Ramón shook his head. The British were quite mad. He recited a prayer to Saint Elmo.

The valley echoed with the din of a tremendous second bellow from the makeshift restored cannon up on the heights. The sound of the gun brought back all the horrors of Trafalgar to young Gloag's mind. His eyes widened. He had seen dreadful things at Trafalgar, sights that would be with him for the rest of his days.

A shot hole appeared in the lateen sail.

Corrie narrowed her eyes. 'More work for your sailmakers, Mr. Jater. Helm, take the Long Reach to Bishop's Spit, and head for Sharpness!'

She was out of range of the Dockyard's ancient gun.

She had done it! She had stolen back her frigate!

Jater would have the damaged sail repaired in the shake of a lamb's tail.

Now Corrie had to find Leisségues's squadron before her crazy brother took on that squadron single-handed. Three years ago, her brother had risked his life for her by taking her place in a duel. Here was a chance to return the favour.

I'm coming, James.

CHAPTER

CORRIE'S BROTHER, Captain James Harriman, commander
of His Majesty's frigate *Belle Poule*, a vessel known affectionately
to those in the Service as *The Pretty Chicken*, had been up before
dawn. James had shaved by the light of a swinging lantern in his
cabin, using his make-do mirror. His helpful ship's carpenter had
reframed the surviving fragment of his personal looking glass
shattered by a splinter during the battle off Cape Trafalgar.

This was his first command. He was determined to make
himself look respectable even in the morning watch. His sister
had always maintained a smart appearance on her Quarter Deck.
He would outdo her. After all, he was a real man whereas she was
merely a woman *pretending* to be a man. Anything she could do,
he could do better. He was a *real* naval officer.

True, his sister had shepherded the entire East India convoy
from the Strait of Malacca halfway around the world and brought
that convoy to London without losing a single vessel. And yes,
cathedral bells had welcomed her to the city! And yes, dammit,
she had been *knighted*.

He leaned closer to the mirror.

Having a sister as successful as Corrie was enough to drive any man crazy.

He scraped off his stubble thoughtfully.

He ran up on deck. He was convoying thirty-four miserable fishing smacks across the Atlantic back to their fishing grounds not far from where he and Corrie had been born. It was too early in the year for such a convoy, but he had been told there was urgency. Something about a French squadron? His mother the admiral worked at the naval station in St. John's. What fun it would be to sail into the Narrows of St. John's Harbour and surprise her, always supposing she was still in command. Perhaps might have accepted a posting somewhere else? It had been years since he had last seen her. He intended to show her that he was *twice* the officer his sister was. He would teach his stuck-up sister a lesson. He would shine in the eyes of his mother. With luck the French squadron, if there rally was a French squadron, would sink some of these stupid fishing boats he was supposed to be guarding. His heart raced at the thought. What a chance at glory! He would exchange broadsides with the French. He would capture a French warship single-handed. He would be awarded hundreds of pounds by a Prize Court. He would see his name in print in the Naval Chronicle. He grabbed his spyglass and dashed to the rail, hoping to sight enemy topsails on the horizon.

He beat his palm with his fist. There was not an enemy in sight. He sighed. His idiot fishing smacks were making no effort to keep together. He was not sure if they even knew how to read his signals. They seemed to be racing one another to be the first over the horizon.

But wait! Something was up! Three of the leading fishing boats were going about and making their way back towards the *Belle Poule* in a hurry. That was promising! Something must have frightened those fishing boats, something they had spied over the curve of the Earth. Those fishing captains had seen something coming up over *their* horizon, something he and his officers had yet to clap eyes on.

James's hopes rose. Was this his chance for glory?

A flicker of distant lightning caught his eye. Dark clouds were massing on the horizon. Perhaps the fishing boats were fleeing from bad weather?

He had to know what was going on. He leaped for the ratlines and scrambled up the rigging. The wind blew his hair across his eyes. The lookout on duty at the foremast cross trees was Bailey.

'What do you see, Bailey?'

'Flashes of white, sir, a-coming and going. Could be seven or eight ships.'

It was hard to focus his glass with the masthead wheeling around in circles.

'Lend me your shoulder, Bailey.'

Her rested the scope on the man's shoulder.

The faraway horizon came and went, came and went. There! He spotted something. A topsail lit up by a flash of lightning.

Aha!

A ship-of-the-line! Part of a British squadron? Or *not*. There was something about that topsail that set his teeth on edge. The topsail looked too bright, too new.

He ran his glass further along the horizon. He spied *another* bright white topsail, and then yet another. Glory be! An entire enemy squadron was hull down and coming up fast. Seven or eight ships, by the look of them, with a storm on their heels. No wonder the fishing boats were racing back for his protection.

'Thank you, Bailey.'

He tucked his telescope back under his arm.

This could be the turning point of my career. Here is my chance to overcome an entire French squadron single-handed!

He had learned a few things from his sister. He had to fool the enemy somehow. He had one thing going for him. His 'Pretty Chicken' was of French design. She looked French. She had been built for the French navy and captured by the British. The set of her sails was French. She could *pass* for French.

He returned to the Quarter Deck in a hurry.

What would Corrie do?

'Mr. Taylor, do we have a French flag?'

'I'm not sure, sir.'

'Find one! Quickly! There is a French squadron bearing down on us. I think they have escaped from Brest. I want to confuse them. I want to make them think we are French. If they think we are French, perhaps they won't open fire on our fishing schooners. They may think our fishing schooners are French, too. I hope they do.'

The Union Jack was lowered.

The flag of the French Revolution was raised in its place.

'Steady as she goes!'

'The French flagship is signalling, sir. Can't read the flags, sir.'

'Raise the Black Ball.'

'The plague flag, captain?'

'Quickly, Jackson. Don't dither.'

'Aye aye, sir. Raising the Black Ball.'

'It is not fooling the Frogs, sir. They are still closing with us. Blimey! Five ships of the line. They'll make mincemeat out of us, captain.'

'Shut your mouth, Jackson. Starboard side guns! Load with round shot. Don't raise the lids until I give the word. Let's hear a song! Give me The Black Ball Line!'

The gunners burst into song:

In the Black Ball Line I served my time
To me way-aye-aye, hurray-ah
And that's the line where you can shine
Hurrah for the Black Ball Line!

The *Belle Poule* and the French flagship *Impérial* were closing with one another rapidly.

A powerful storm was overtaking them both.

Now James could see the faces of the French officers on the Quarter Deck of the *Impérial*. He spotted a French midshipman pointing at the Black Ball and gesticulating, and saw the French captain shake his head.

James experienced a sinking feeling in his stomach. His mind froze.

If Corrie were here, what would she do?

'Haul down the French colours. Hoist our own! Hard over, helm! Steer close under the Frenchman's stern. Starboard gunners! Raise your lids! Run out! Fire as you bear!'

One by one the starboard guns of the *Belle Poule* went into action, shaking the air with the sounds of their discharges while sending round after round smashing into the captain's cabin of the French ship-of-the-line. James heard the French shouting in anger. He saw French fire parties rushing with buckets of seawater to quench the flames.

James gulped. He had made his first hit. But now what?

Which way would the *Impérial* veer to bring to bring *her* guns to bear? To port or to starboard?

He heard the enemy captain shout an order. He saw the enemy helmsman spin his wheel. He saw the bows of the *Impérial* begin to turn.

Without warning something thumped heavily into the Belle Poule's vulnerable side, and enemy boarders came swarming aboard.

James gasped.

He drew his sword.

There was a tremendous crash of thunder right overhead. A pig in the ship's manger squealed.

Boarders! A thrust to the breastbone! A quick parry! James stepped back and made a feint the left. He stamped hard on a Frenchman's foot.

He swung around. He had to make a riposte. His brain raced.

I shall win this battle against impossible odds. My report to the Admiralty will make for fine reading in the Naval Chronicle.

If Corrie could see me now…

A Frenchman hit him on the head.

8

CHAPTER

CORRIE WAS EAGER to try out her newly built galley with its eighteen oars at the earliest opportunity. Could her galley could move fast enough upwind? How many men and women could it carry? How would it fare in a dead calm?

Her steward Harbottle came climbing up the companionway step by step carrying a tray. His captain might be hungry and thirsty.

She waved him away. 'Not now, Harbottle!'

Harbottle nodded, turned and began to limp back down to the captain's galley, still balancing the tray. Going down the steps was more difficult for his wounded leg that going up the steps.

A fierce gale had carried the *Swift* clear across the Channel and into the Bay of Biscay. Corrie could see several French vessels hugging the coast.

'Those c-coasters will be carrying supplies for the French army,' volunteered Lieutenant Partridge. 'That is the mouth of the Gironde. I was here with Captain Harmood. We could never get close enough to catch the inshore t-traffic. There are many rocks hereabouts, captain, and treacherous t-tides.'

'Understood,' replied Corrie. 'Thank you, Mr. Partridge. Mr. Jensen! I want fish for my supper.'

'Aye aye, cap'n. That fishing boat off our port bow has just taken in her nets. She's low in water. I'd say she has a big catch.'

'Bring us alongside. You speak French, Mr. Partridge?'

'Yes, sir.'

The skipper of the fishing smack was deeply suspicious when she entered Corrie's cabin. She feared to lose her boat *and* her catch to these perfidious British. Fishing boats were supposed to be immune from seizure. Was she to be made prisoner? She had no wish to rot in a foreign jail. She was a *fisherwoman*, plain and simple, and not some revolutionary officer in the *marine française.*

Corrie saw the alarm in the fisherwoman eyes. Corrie felt for her.

'A glass of rum for our visitor, Mr. Partridge. Pour one for yourself as well.'

'I don't d-drink, c-captain.'

'Pretend you do, Mr. Partridge. Clink glasses with the fishing boat skipper. Tell her we are very sorry but we have to impound her catch.'

The fisherwoman said something about her family and the price of bread.

Partridge turned to Corrie. 'She is anxious.'

'Tell her we will pay market price for her catch.'

A gleam came into the fishing captain's eye. So she understood *some* English. That was interesting.

'Ask her how much her catch is worth,' said Corrie, going to her desk and unlocking her strongbox.

'She says it is worth two twenty-franc gold pieces.'

'Offer her instead this George III guinea. Tell her that it is made of solid gold.' She passed the coin to Partridge.

The fishing skipper gazed solemnly at the gold coin. She placed the coin between her teeth and bit it. It was gold all right. Such a coin would buy a month's food for her family.

The fisherwoman removed the coin from her mouth and then held it tightly in one hand. She was wise in the ways of the world. She knew she had to earn this gold. She knew this good-for-nothing English son-of-a-bitch wanted something from her in return.

'Ask her if there are any French navy ships hereabouts.'

The fishing skipper waved one arm expressively as she replied.

'She says there are two brigs moored upriver, but there is a guard-ship patrolling the river mouth.'

Corrie clapped the woman on her shoulder. 'Mr. Partridge, give our guest another drink. The moment we have her catch stowed below decks, see her safely back to her fishing boat. For now, talk to her.'

'What do I t-talk about?' asked Partridge, at a loss for words.

'Anything you wish,' said Corrie, locking her strongbox and leaving the cabin.

Two brigs moored upriver! A guard ship!

'Bosun Ballwright!'

'Captain?'

'Launch the galley.'

'Aye aye, captain.'

'Mr. Keeper! Muster one hundred hands. Our best rowers at the oars. A weapon for every man and woman. You are in command. Jeanette is your second. Take off your uniform jacket.

Hide it under a thwart. There is a guard ship at the river mouth and there are two brigs moored somewhere upriver. Do as much damage as you can. Return by dawn. Any questions?'

'None, sir.'

Corrie watched one hundred of her people crowd into the forty-foot galley. Fraser Keeper ordered them all to lie down flat on top of one another. There were bawdy jokes as her people did was they were told.

'In all my years I have never ever seen the like!' said old Mr. Weevil, staring down into the packed galley.

Corrie was deliberately giving Fraser and Jeanette a chance to recover their self-confidence after what they had both endured during the battle off Cape Trafalgar.

She raised her voice to harangue the cutting-out party. 'In London I watched rowers compete for Doggett's Coat and Badge. The rowers started from London Bridge and rowed all the way to Chelsea. Boy! You should have seen them row! They rowed *like smoke*. Crowds lined the banks of the river, cheering them on. I want you to fool the French in their guard ship. I want you to stop rowing, rest on your oars, and wave at the French cheerfully! Make the French think that you are *rowing for fun*. Let's rehearse. Give me a wave right now, you oarsmen! Go on! You can do better than that! Now let's see you *smile!* That's much better. Now give me a cheer!'

'Three cheers for Captain Harriman! Hip, hip…hurrah! Hip, hip…hurrah! Hip, hip…hurrah!'

'Good! Off you go and capture that guard ship! Cast off when ready!'

Lieutenant Fraser Keeper nodded. 'Ready, steady… pull! Keep her going! Put your backs into it!'

Under oars, the brand-new galley made her way upwind at a truly extraordinary pace, heading straight for the French guard ship they could see more than a mile away. The guard ship was busy patrolling the mouth of the river.

'We have very few hands on board to work the ship,' said Anne quietly.

Corrie grinned. 'We won't tell the French.'

Corrie put her glass to her eye. She focused on the enemy guard ship. A bunch of French seamen had crowded the rail. A French officer had come to see what the fuss was about. The officer did not seem to be alarmed. He could have no idea just how many British raiders were hidden out of sight on the bottom-boards of the galley.

The galley was nearing the guard ship now.

Would Lieutenant Keeper remember to put the French off their guard?

She heard Keeper give a low-voiced command. She saw the galley rowers rest on their oars. She saw them wave cheerfully at the enemy. She saw the crew of the French guard ship wave back, quite unsuspecting. Her ruse was working. The French had no idea what was about to hit them.

'The fish are all aboard, sir, and the fishing skipper is safely back aboard her own vessel.'

'Three sails on the horizon, captain,' sang out Billy Brown suddenly.

Corrie spun on her heel to have a look. 'Captains of the Tops to the Quarter Deck!' she cried.

Billy Brown, the Captain of the Maintop, came sliding down the stay. She was the first to arrive. 'Coo deh, cap'n!' she said.

Billy was joined moments later by both Popham, Captain of the Mizzen, and Chaffet, Captain of the Fore.

Corrie looked the three over and addressed them quietly. 'Captains of the Tops, we have a problem. Those are French sails on the horizon. They don't know we have only a few dozen hands on board. I want us to frighten them. I want to make them think we are *fully manned* and *eager to take them on*. Suggestions?'

'We big up ourselves, cap'n,' said Billy, her white teeth gleaming in her dark face.

'What do you mean, Billy?'

'We head straight for de enemy. We drop all sails one time. Foremast, Mainmast, Mizzen. All one time. What enemy think? '

Corrie's eyes narrowed. 'The enemy will think we have *a full crew*. But can you do that?'

Billy nodded. 'Tie all sails with yarn. Cut yarn all same time.'

Corrie's face lit up. 'Brilliant, Billy! Absolutely brilliant!'

'You give order, we cut yarn,' said Billy.

The other two captains of the Tops nodded.

'Make it so,' said Corrie, and she bit her lip.

Her men and women dashed out along the yards, removing the heavy lashings that held the bundled canvas in place and replacing the lashings with thin yarn easy to cut in a hurry.

'Helm, head as straight for the enemy corvettes as this wind will allow.'

'Aye, aye, cap'n,' said her steersman, and spun the wheel.

The *Swift* turned to face the three oncoming French warships.

'All fruits ripe, cap'n.'

'Sever those yarns!'

All the *Swift*'s sails fell into place rapidly as if they had been cast off from their gaskets by fifty hands.

The canvas caught the wind and filled.

The *Swift* leaned over sharply, and gathered speed. The water under her forefoot made itself heard.

Corrie stood with one knee bent to make up for the sudden cant of the deck, and watched her enemies closely.

The sound of water under the *Swift*'s forefoot grew louder and louder.

It was a bluff.

Would the French fall for it?

Spray hit Corrie's face. She wiped her brow with her kerchief.

She made an attempt to push the terrifying memories of that battle off Cape Trafalgar to the back of her mind. Images of slaughter and mayhem haunted her. Only last night she had cried out in her sleep, thrashed around, and then woken up in a blind panic. Tom had said he had heard her calling out to her father! Her father Archibald had not been seen since that fight. He was among the many missing and unaccounted for. She missed him greatly.

This bluff of hers had better work.

The French have seen us make sail on all three masts at once. Will they be fooled? Will they think we have a full crew. I hope they do.

There came a shout from the masthead. It was young Ramón. '*Mi capitana!* The enemy they turn away!'

Thank heavens!

The three enemy corvettes were headed for the shore.

'Man the bow-chaser.'

'Yes, c-captain,' said Mr. Partridge. 'Maximum elevation! Ball shot!'

The range was too great for a hit, but the sound of their gun might frighten the French. It was worth making the effort.

'Fire!'

'All three enemy ships are still heading for the shore,' said Mr. Weevil, pounded his palm with his fist. 'They are sure to run aground, captain.'

Corrie nodded. 'We had better stand off. Haul our wind! If the enemy coasters can get close enough to the beach, their crews will try to swim for it. One corvette has run aground already! Helm hard over! See if you can sink her.'

The bow-chaser fired again and again.

'Aye, aye, c-captain.'

There were distant shouts of despair from the French.

Corrie saw figures thrashing about in the waves.

It was a sorry sight.

'The other enemy coasters have run aground too, *mi capitana*!' came a triumphant shout from the masthead.

'Redirect your fire! Try to sink all three. WE can be sure they are crammed with supplies intended for Napoleon's *Grand Armée*! Let's send those supplies to the bottom!'

Napoleon's soldiers needed those provisions to help them fight the Prussians. By far the fastest way to feed Napoleon's troops was to deliver supplies to his soldiers by ship. But now, after Trafalgar, the British ruled the seas. Now naval power would make a real and telling difference.

Corrie felt sorry for the French sailors thrashing about in the water. She herself could not swim. She had nearly drowned at Trafalgar. By their antics she judged that many of the French could swim no better than she. It was heart-breaking to watch them drown, but these inshore waters were too treacherous to risk salvage. Perhaps some of the swimmers would make it ashore. She sincerely hoped so.

'Ready about! Back to the mouth of the river. We must rendezvous with our galley.'

'I thought you had forgotten all about the away party,' said Anne softly. She was the mother of Lieutenant Keeper, the officer commanding the cutting-out expedition.

'Not for one moment,' replied Corrie gently. 'We may need our galley when we meet that squadron of ships-of-the-line your spy tells us Napoleon has ordered out into the Atlantic. I hope my brother has not met that squadron already.'

The *Swift* raced back to the mouth of the Gironde estuary.

What had become of their raiding party?

It had grown dark.

The Moon had risen.

Corrie remembered how the expedition had begun. She had peered through her telescope. She had seen Lieutenant Keeper bring his crowded galley within shouting distance of the enemy guard ship. She had seen the crew of the galley wave to the enemy to put them off guard.

Then she had seen Keeper launch his attack.

She had seen Keeper scramble up the side of the guard ship. She had heard someone fire a pistol. She had heard cries of dismay from the French. She had seen her people swarm up over the side on the guard ship.

That was all she had been able to see and hear clearly before the corvettes had been sighted and she had had to leave the scene in a hurry.

How had Fraser managed in the interim? Had his attack succeeded?

Was he still alive?

Was Jeanette still alive?

'I hope they are all right,' she muttered, mirroring Anne's concern.

She recalled how Fraser had jumped over the bodies of the wounded, freed his blade from its scabbard and dashed along the deck of the guard ship.

No doubt Fraser had done his best to keep his mind focused on finding the guard boat's captain and forcing that man or woman to surrender.

But she knew Fraser had felt somewhat uncertain of himself of late.

And the love of his life Jeanette, too, was an unknown quantity.

The battle off Cape Trafalgar had left both of them disfigured. Fraser had told her in confidence that his heart tended to beat fast, and then slow. Apparently he had killed several people during that dreadful battle near Cape Trafalgar. He had confessed to being unsure of his own name after the engagement came to an end. Had Corrie been wrong to put him in charge of the away mission? Had she been wrong to appoint Jeanette as his second-in-command? She would have to wait for Fraser's report to hear his story…

9

CHAPTER

FRASER encountered the enemy captain emerging from his cabin, and then, seeing how bewildered his enemy looked, tried to make it easy on the poor fellow.

'We outnumber your crew ten to one, captain,' Fraser said in simple schoolroom French. 'Do you surrender, monsieur?'

The bewildered Frenchman spread his arms wide. He gazed about him in astonishment. His jaw dropped. Why, his entire vessel was swarming with British mariners! *Putain de merde!* Where had they all come from? Why had he not been informed? But certainly this was... a fait accompli!

'The ship she is yours. I surrender,' the Frenchman said quickly, and then, true to his word, the fellow reversed his sword and handed his personal weapon to Fraser before running to the side of his guard ship to look down. *Mon dieu!* A *huge galley* lay alongside. The galley was as large as a small cutter! His jaw dropped. But this was incredible! Surely it was not possible! He had never seen a galley so big. Where had this galley come from?

Fraser pulled himself together. 'Please tell your people to lay down their arms, captain. Tell them we shall set them ashore unharmed. I will set you ashore with them. That is a promise. I give you my word as a gentleman. Here, have your sword back!'

The bewildered French captain of the guard ship returned his sword to its scabbard and raised his voice to address his hard-pressed crew in a broad Bordeaux accent. 'Lay down your arms!' he hollered. 'We go ashore! We shall not be prisoners!' He made these extravagant promises in the hope that the British *lieutenant de vaisseau* with the ravaged face would be true to his word. *Hélas!* What else could he do? These insidious British left him no choice.

Fraser Keeper raised his voice to address his own people. 'Cease firing, everybody! Round up and confine our French prisoners! Tend to the wounded! Jeanette! Where are you?'

'Over here,' replied that muscular young woman from the isle of Sark who had been so badly scalded by molten lead.

She waved at him and grinned.

'This ship has guns, Jeanette. Load them!'

Jeanette ran to examine the guard ship's armament. 'They don't use flintlocks,' she reported, surprised. ' They have a slow match burning in a tub. I need experienced gunners.'

'Croutear, Dormer, Davis, Brown and you, too, Wilson! Help Jeanette load and run out! There are two enemy brigs somewhere up this river. We must find and destroy them.'

The gunners cast about to find cartridges while Sergeant Deering and his marines rounded up the bewildered members of the French crew.

'Laykin! Up the mast with you. Sing out if you see anything!'

Fraser grabbed the huge tiller of the guard ship. He threw his weight on it. 'Ready about!' he shouted.

The guard boat answered to her helm. Her boom swung over, narrowly missing Jeanette. The canvas caught the wind. The ship heeled. Her bow wave parted the waters of the river, stirring the reeds on both shores. Towing the galley in her wake, the guard boat headed up the estuary in search of enemy brigs, if in truth there were any brigs to be found.

The moon rose higher and higher above the horizon, turning the waters silver. The reflections of a million moons danced in their wake. It became an absurdly romantic scene, and he and Jeanette exchanged fond glances. What a night to make babies together!

He grinned.

She grinned.

All at once Fraser felt better. Much better. More himself. More like the person he had been *before* the horrors of Trafalgar.

'Lieutenant!' Laykin whispered from the masthead. 'Two brigs moored close to the shore.'

'Thanks,' Fraser whispered back.

Minutes later Fraser spied the brigs for himself, lit up by the moon.

Both vessels had been moored by their bows leaving their vulnerable sterns open to attack. 'Fire when ready, Jeanette!' he said, leaning on the tiller to coax the guard ship around and bring the guns to bear.

'Fire!' cried Jeanette.

The guns fired, filling the night air with smoke that made Fraser's eyes smart, and then had to be sponged out to remove debris, reloaded, and rolled forward from the recoil.

Fraser heard a despairing cry from the nearest brig. Perhaps the crews of both brigs had gone ashore, leaving a single sentinel to keep anchor watch.

He swung the guard ship about to make another pass. The guns thundered again. This time there was no answering cry.

Both vessels caught fire.

It was pitiful to see.

One brig keeled over.

The other exploded.

A lucky shot had found her powder store.

Fraser cursed. The noise of that explosion would alert the authorities at the river mouth. The French might try to get a boom across. It was high time to bring this raid to an end. He only hoped that he had not left it too late to retreat?

'Cease firing! Man the galley! Ferry the prisoners ashore in small groups.'

Putting the woman and men prisoners ashore took an hour. Fraser grew more and more worried. He was deep in enemy territory, and it was growing light with the approach of dawn.

As they landed the French prisoners, their enemies shouted insults, and shook their fists at the cowardly British who had stolen their ship by means of a ruse.

Able seaman John Eaves lost his temper. 'Bloody Frogs!' he shouted back.

'Watch your mouth, Eaves!'

'Sorry, sir,' said Eaves, but he did not sound at all sorry.

Last of all to be put ashore was the captain of the guard ship.

Suddenly the wind veered.

Fraser tacked back and forth across the slowly wending river, anxious to get back to sea before French artillery showed up to prevent his return to the Bay of Biscay.

Another anxious hour passed before they returned to the mouth of the river, their faithful galley in tow and bobbing behind them.

Fraser tensed. Was that a boom he saw slung across the river mouth to prevent their escape?

No! Thank heavens! It was not! It was merely the trunk of a fallen tree that had been washed down the river to the sea after a storm.

Fraser exhaled.

He reached out for held Jeanette's hand in the half-light.

They looked into one another's eyes.

This had been their lucky night!

They felt better. They let go of one another. It would be bad for discipline for the pair to be seen comforting one another. Intimacy would have to wait until later, if ever they had the chance to be alone together for more than a moment or two. Romance was far from easy to manage on a crowded frigate.

They sailed the captured guard ship out into the bay, using the offshore wind that had sprung up earlier.

They searched the horizon eagerly for any sign of their frigate the *Swift*.

No sign.

What had become of their beloved frigate?

'She is gone,' said the Welshman Laykin, crestfallen.

But before long a spark of dawn sunlight appeared on the far horizon. A vessel was approaching.

Was the vessel theirs?

They craned their necks to see.

'That is the *Swift*,' announced Jeanette. She had keenest eyes.

The crew cheered.

What a relief!

'Haul down the French ensign and raise our own.'

Two hours later the *Swift* slid alongside the guard ship.

'Fenders!' Mr. Weevil shouted.

The raiding party, jubilant but very tired after their long night up the enemy river, made their way aboard, chattering volubly.

Fraser saluted Corrie. He made his report.

'Two brigs sunk. No prisoners. No casualties. No damage to the galley.' He made no mention of his personal doubts. He did say a word to Corrie about the moment when he had faced the enemy captain. That would remain private, and would be with him for the rest of his life. The ruse had worked. They had greatly outnumbered the French. Fraser might have ordered all the French *matelots* killed and thrown overboard. He had considered doing so. Such slaughter would have saved time and been far less risky than being merciful. But his decision to save those enemy lives was no part of his report. Reports had to be brief, factual, and unemotional. That was the tradition in the Navy. For the first time in his life, Fraser appreciated the *wisdom* of that tradition. There was much that Fraser had no wish at all to tell his captain. He was pretty sure his captain, with years of experience behind her, could fill in the details for herself.

'Well done, Mr. Keeper!' was all that Corrie said. She was indeed wise enough to guess at what Fraser had left unsaid.

She turned to her Sailing Master. 'Mr. Weevil. Have our galley hoisted aboard the *Swift* and stowed securely. Our galley has served us well, and may serve us again.'

Her people gave a cheer when she said that.

Corrie was pleased with success of her little raid. The huge sum of her own money she had paid for the galley had paid off. With luck. the captured guard ship would bring in a tidy sum in prize money. She made the calculation in her head. Her captain's share when awarded by an Admiralty Prize Court would be two eighths. That more than enough to recompense her for the galley.

It was at moments like this that she missed her father. He would have made her laugh about it.

In the past, her father's advice when it came to matters of prize money and navy politics had been invaluable. She would have found her father's advice useful today. But of course she had heard no word of Archibald since the day she had sent him aboard that French warship as prize master!

A depressing thought came unbidden into her mind.

My father must be dead.

10

CHAPTER

CORRIE'S FATHER, Lieutenant Archibald Harriman, *knew* he was dead.

He could hear the Chair of the Parliamentary Committee for the Design of The Next World firing questions at him: 'What was it like being a monkey? Did you feel responsible for the animals you ate? What exactly was a *religion*?'

Before he could begin to answer these searching questions, Archibald began to think that perhaps he was not quite as dead as he thought.

He could hear the creaking of a ship's hull expanding and contracting with the stresses of wind and weather. Why, he could even hear orders being shouted, and bare feet pounding the deck!

Puzzled, he opened his eyes.

It was dark.

Strange shapes were scurrying here and there.

Was this the Afterlife?

Or was he, perhaps, aboard the *Bellerophon*?

He could feel the ship pitching to heavy seas. He felt a sudden jerk as she was brought up short by a towline. Yes, this *must* be

the *Bellerophon*. He winced. If his memory served him right, the
Bellerophon was towing the dismasted *Temeraire* to Gibraltar for
emergency repairs. The *Temeraire* had come to their rescue during
the battle, so now they were doing their best to try and save the
98-gun second-rate. That was laudable, but oh, how it hurt! Every
jerk of that towline sent stabs of pain through his wounded leg.
He could feel and hear his broken bones grate together!. HE
became aware of the passage of time. He must have been lying
here in this cot under this damned half-deck for *days on end*. No
wonder it was driving him crazy! No wonder he had thought he
was dead! Being dead would be far, far better than this.

A couple of fellow officers paused by his hammock to say a
few kind words to him in an effort to keep up his spirits. Damn
their eyes! Why could they not leave him alone?

'They'll soon put you to rights at Gibraltar Hospital,' said one
cheerful idiot.

'Don't worry. They'll save your leg,' said some confounded fool.

While he was grateful to his colleagues for their unbounded
optimism, their voices began to sound faraway and strange to
his ears, and after a while the great pain from the jerking of the
ship became too much to bear, and he slid back into emptiness.
He had seen a certain vacant look in the eyes of others who had
been severely wounded. Perhaps that same sense of foreboding
was overcoming him? He vowed not to let himself die of gloom.
There was hope. He had studied the chart. Gibraltar was not *that*
far away. In *three days* at most he would be taken ashore and then
perhaps the world would stop heaving and jerking and maybe,
just maybe, he would have a little peace in which to attempt a
recovery.

Three days later his wish came true.

He became aware of being carried ashore on a stretcher, probably one of a long line of wounded women, men and children.

They deposited him none too gently on an unmoving bed.

Ouch!

Many hours passed before Archibald woke from a fitful slumber to find himself in a ward crawling with flies. Flies were thick on the ceiling. Flies tickled his face. Flies crawled about on his blanket, attracted by the blood. His fever worsened. He saw disembodied heads floating in the air. He cried aloud in a waking dream. For a while he was sure he was playing football. He swung his wounded leg this way and that, undoing all of the patient work of the surgeon who had carefully aligned his bones so that they might knit together properly, and then, in a rare moment of clarity Archibald became aware that those who were supposed to be caring for him were holding some kind of an emergency conference to decide what to do with him next!

'Don't saw my leg off!' he told them sternly.

The surgeon broke away from the consultation and came the bedside to speak to him. 'We shall not saw your leg off, lieutenant. Instead, we shall lock your wounded limb up in a *leg-box* for nine days. That will give your bones time to facilitate the formation of callus.'

A carpenter was sent for to build him a leg-box.

His leg was straightened out. The broken bones were realigned. His leg was put in the box. The box was nailed shut with a hammer. Ouch, ouch, ouch! *That* hurt!

Six days passed.

In the middle of the sixth night, something quite unexpected happened.

An elderly nurse who was supposed to be looking after Archibald decided to smoke her pipe. Apparently smoking while on duty was against the hospital rules. When the nurse heard someone coming, she thrust the smoldering pipe into her pocket to avoid discovery. Shortly after that the old woman fell asleep, her pipe forgotten, and the burning tobacco set fire to her petticoat.

Archibald woke to find himself coughing.

The ward was full of smoke!

He hauled himself out of bed as handily as he could, dragging his leg-box behind him.

He used his bed rug to smother the flames.

He saved the nurse's life.

Next morning Archibald felt something odd going on *inside his leg-box*. He became convinced that a mouse was nibbling the calf of his leg. His fever lessened. His head began to clear. He drew his dirk and slid the blade inside the leg-box over and over again in an effort to try to relieve the pain. Ouch! What was going on? Had scorpions had made a nest in his bandages? It was simply *maddening*.

On the ninth day, his doctors crowded round to see his leg-box opened. Apparently the sawbones were as eager as himself to discover what had been irritating him so.

His leg-box was pried open and disassembled.

He had his leg back!

His fellow patients in the ward gasped.

He gazed down at his leg in horror.

What a sight! Hundreds of maggots were burrowing into his calf. Only the tips of their wriggling tails could be seen.

The surgeons exchanged knowing glances. They called for forceps. One by one the maggots were removed. Then his leg was soused in a strange and foul-smelling potion.

'Lieutenant Harriman,' said the surgeon. 'Get up and walk!'

The surgeon had to be out of his mind!

'Walk? Are you sure?' Archibald croaked.

The surgeon nodded.

Archibald bit his lip. 'Very well. I'll try.'

He swung his legs over the side of the bed.

Will my bad leg work?

Gingerly, he let both legs take his weight.

His wounded leg supported his weight! A callus had formed. The maggots had cleaned his wound.

He shook hands enthusiastically with his doctors.

'Thank you,' he said, with tears in his eyes. 'Thank you so much. You have saved my leg.'

'Exercise every day,' was the advice. 'The more you exercise, the stronger your wounded leg will become.'

'I shall exercise,' he promised, and then hobbled over to the window of the ward to look out over the Bay of Gibraltar.

He saw a pod of dolphins leaping through the waves.

Tears wet his face as he watched the dolphins frolic.

His thoughts focused on what to do next.

I'm going to make it. If only I had some way to reach my wife and let her know that I survived the engagement off Cape Trafalgar, but I am told that all outgoing mails have been cancelled. Apparently a lethal miasmic contagion has spread through the garrison here in Gibraltar, and quarantine measures are in force. The sending of letters has been strictly forbidden.

I think I had better escape from this hospital as fast as I can hobble.

He took great care not to touch the handle of the hospital door as he left the building. The surgeon who had fixed his leg had warned him that the malignant fever was spreading rapidly. The Lieutenant-Governor of Gibraltar, General Charles O'Hara, had vomited blood, developed a high fever, and died. The Lieutenant-Governor's tongue had turned white with a brown streak, the surgeon had been eager to say, a detail that Archibald could have done without.

Now Archibald was leaving the hospital in a hurry.

It felt good to be out in the open air again, limping down the hill to DeRolle's Regimental Barracks. Before the battle, Nelson had forbade *any* of his people to go ashore here in Gibraltar for fear they might infect the fleet. If his memory served, Nelson had ordered DeRolle's Regiment *disbanded*. How very extraordinary! Had *all* of the DeRolle's soldiers died of this miserable contagion?

His newly-healed leg hurt. He leaned against the wall of the Garrison Library for a moment to get his breath back. Distant wails of anguish could be heard coming from a collection of jumbled sheds down by the waterfront where the poor lived in squalor. He felt sorry for the wretches. No hospitals for the uneducated. They would all die. Their bodies would be thrown into a mass grave.

The scuttlebutt was that this latest outbreak of whatever-it-was had begun right here in this Garrison Library and then spread downhill. Sooner or later the plague would affect the entire town.

Why, the *Gibraltar Chronicle* had been forced to cease publication for lack of staff! And incoming mail was being landed on lazaretto ships, permanently anchored out in the Bay. Every letter and every packet had to be handled with tongs and wiped with vinegar.

The screams and moans of the plague victims grew louder as Archibald limped on down the hill towards the waterfront.

The sooner I leave Gibraltar the safer I'll feel. It could be months before the Admiralty gives me a fresh posting. I would be very surprised to learn that anyone even knows that I survived the recent battle off Cape Trafalgar. I am sure my children do not know, and I doubt very much if my wife has had any news of me for years. Surely my family thinks me done for.

He limped on down the hill, conscious of the Rock of Gibraltar rearing up into the sky behind him. He heard the chatter of a strange creature. Something fast and hairy nearly knocked him off his feet. So Gibraltar had wild animals? How interesting. He wondered what sort of animals they were.

He paused to catch his breath. His wounded leg was a nuisance. It slowed him down.

I have to exercise. My doctor told me so.

He arrived at the docks.

Many small craft were moored there.

He spotted several of the schooners that had helped ferry the wounded ashore after the engagement. Now those schooners were forbidden to sail for fear they might spread the disease to other ports.

He hobbled along, examining each moored craft in turn. Here was a fishing boat from Portugal, and here…he must be seeing things… was this really a vessel from his own homeland of Newfoundland?

He stared hungrily at the graceful gaff-rigged fishing schooner. She was a beauty! She was built of pine, spruce, birch and oak. She had two sturdy masts more than a hundred feet high. He judged that she would have a crew of about twenty. Several hands could be seen at work on deck. One fellow was sorting fish he had spread out to dry. He was culling the fish into four qualities while spinning a yarn to amuse the ship's boy.

'You better be good, Tommy Decker,' Archibald heard the old fellow say, 'Or the Bully Boo'll be here after the Boo Man.'

'And then the Lopchops will snap you up,' Archibald added in his broadest Newfoundland accent.

Archibald had in his youth made trips to the Southern Shore in a schooner very like this one. In fact he had started out as a twelve-year-old of about the same age as this young pucklin who was listening tongue-in-cheek to the culler's tale and doing his best not to grin. When you are twelve years of age, *everything* is funny.

The culler looked up sharply at the sound of Archibald's voice. 'A Newlander?' he asked, staring at Archibald curiously.

Archibald held the fellow's gaze. 'How many Green Men have you?' he asked.

The fellow tossed one more salt cod into his pile of Second Bests, and then stood up straight to brush off his cuffs. He cast a more searching eye over this stranger standing on the dock. 'You'll be wanting a word with the skipper?' he said, and frowned. 'And you a cripple?' he added, staring at Archibald's wounded leg.

Archibald looked the man up and down, daring him to say one word more.

The sorter of fish seemed to think better of that, and sang out to his captain. 'Fella to see you, skipper!'

The master of the schooner *Marie Spindler* came up on deck, wiping whale oil from his hands with a scrap of cloth. Evidently he had been filling his lamps.

The master eyed Archibald keenly.

'A navy man?' he asked, spotting the brass buttons on Archibald's jacket.

'Lieutenant Harriman, from St. John's. Stranded after the battle. Looking for a ride home.'

The master of the schooner shook his head. 'Wish I could help you, Lieutenant. I lost my brother to this cursed fever. A fine fellow for charts was my brother. Never could make head nor tail of them myself. You do know that we are not *allowed* to sail?'

'Yes, I do,' Archibald replied quietly. 'Do you have a sextant?'

Many fishing boats trusted more to luck and keeping an eye on the weather to find their way about the world.

The captain of the schooner said 'Yes, my son. I have a sextant. You'd have to work your passage. Takes two awful men to heave out the bunt of a seine. How's that leg of yourn?' he asked, pointing with his finger.

'On the mend,' Archibald replied. 'If I could have a look at your sextant and study your chart, Captain...?'

'Chaffey is my name. Come aboard! Watch out for our moocher! Be careful you don't squat our pet mouse or our lad will be have a thing or two to say to you.'

Archibald lowered himself down into the *Marie Spindler*'s cuddy. On the way down he met the ship's boy's pet mouse face to face, and the creature gazed at him hopefully with its bright little eyes, hoping for a treat.

A fellow stowaway, Archibald thought. 'Later,' he whispered to the mouse.

Archibald knew he could get into big trouble with the law for helping stranded fisherfolk. He went over in his head all that he knew about Green Men. The Act to Encourage the Trade to Newfoundland had been given royal assent by King William. The original intent of the act had been to *discourage* the carrying of passengers to Newfoundland, and to *encourage* fishermen native to England, Wales and Berwick-on-Tweed to trade with and to fish in Newfoundland waters, but *not* to build themselves homes in Newfoundland. But that had been a hundred years ago. Since that passing of that Act, a tradition had grown up allowing a few hands to flaunt the regulations and overwinter in the 'fishing rooms' and to guard valuable gear, boats and supplies. These fellows were known to skippers like Chaffey as 'Green Men.'

Archibald knew that any stretch of the Newfoundland coast where there were sheds built for the drying of fish qualified as a 'room.' The captain of the first fishing boat to arrive at a particular stretch of Newfoundland coast in the spring of the year became the 'Lord' or 'Admiral' of that particular room for that season. By this unofficial arrangement, one in every six members of a fishing schooner's crew was allowed to be a 'Green Man' and be ferried across the Atlantic simply to help with the plantings and help feed those brave few who did overwinter. Perhaps this custom might serve Archibald's purpose, if Captain Chaffey were to agree to take him on as a Green Man. Coffey needed a navigator. But was his sextant in working order? Was his chart, probably copied from Captain Cook's excellent survey of Newfoundland's coastal waters, up to date? Archibald very much hoped so.

Down in the cabin, he examined the sextant carefully, and breathed a sigh of relief. Yes, the instrument was in good fettle.

Then he examined the skipper's chart of the Atlantic and found it recent, and annotated.

His hopes rose.

'I can navigate you to St. John's if you are willing to run the blockade. I might even be able to help you bluff your way out.'

Captain Chaffey's face lit up.

The ship's mouse scurried across the chart table.

The ship's boy scooped up the mouse with one deft swipe of his hand.

'What's your name, lad?' Archibald asked.

'Tommy,' the boy replied.

'Do you know how to keep very quiet and not say a word or make a noise?'

The boy nodded with saying a word. His look made very clear what he thought of strangers who treated him as if he were a *child* and asked him *silly questions*.

Smart cracky.

That very night, under cover of darkness, the fishing schooner *Marie Spindler* slipped quietly though the sheltered waters off the New Mole, taking advantage of a backdraft from the Rock of Gibraltar.

Lieutenant Archibald Harriman held a finger to his lips to remind young Tommy to keep as quiet as his mouse.

The twelve-year-old nodded to show he understood perfectly well and needed *no* reminder, and then scrambled barefoot up on deck to hold up his mouse up in the air so that the creature might see how excitingly dark it was, and sniff the night air and enjoy the smells of spinach tortilla and Karantita wafting from the town.

It was pretty dark. The lanterns in the King's Bastion were reflected in the dancing waters of the bay. A gust of hot air stirred the limbs of the trees on Windmill Hill.

The schooner was almost invisible on a night like this. Would she be stopped by the navy's quarantine patrol?

'Now!' whispered Captain Chaffey by way of a warning.

A block rattled. The boom went over. Archibald ducked his head. On the very next tack they would be able to clear the New Mole, if they were not arrested before they got there.

Archibald's plan was to clear the New Mole, and then head across the bay of Rosia leaving Europa Point well behind them. There would be a lookout stationed atop the Rock who would be able to see for miles come the dawn. So they would have to be well over the horizon by then.

Would this wind persist?

If they became becalmed while evading the blockade, they be captured and reprimanded. The schooner would be impounded and her gear confiscated. The Navy was very strict indeed about quarantine. Archibald bit his lip. What they were attempting was a big risk, but what else could he do? If they remained in Gibraltar Harbour, surely they would all die of the contagion. On the other hand, if they could just slip past the navy guard boat on the dark night, then he and the crew of the *Marie Spindler* and the cracky's mouse might yet live to see the Narrows of St. John's Harbour on the far side of the Atlantic, where his beloved wife, Admiral Wentworth, awaited him. Now there was a prospect to warm the cockles of a man's heart!

There came a sudden splash from somewhere close-by, followed by a curse. Had they been spotted? Archibald held his breath and waited.

He heard the squeak, squeak, squeak of oars being worked in ungreased rowlocks. The sound grew louder and louder.

A craft was coming nearer and nearer.

A navy guard boat.

Archibald heard the voice of the officer in charge of the guard boat reprimand one of his men. Yes, it was the quarantine patrol! Archibald's heart sank. The patrol sounded close! Too close for comfort!

A challenging voice came out of the blackness.

'What ship are you?'

Archibald had to reply. He exchanged glances with the ship's boy.

He cupped his hands around his mouth to make his voice carry. 'Good evening, Midshipman Paisley!' he said loudly. 'Your rowlocks need greasing! I could hear you coming half a mile way. Can't you keep your men keep quieter than that? You're supposed to making it *difficult* for those trying to elude the blockade, not *easier*!'

There came an immediate and angry retort from the guard boat. 'My name is not Paisley, and I'm not a midshipman. Now answer my challenge: What ship are you?'

Archibald had to act the part of *a puzzled senior officer*. 'I thought Paisley was on duty tonight? Did he go down with the plague?'

In real life, Archibald had exchanged yarns with Midshipman Paisley. Paisley had occupied the cot next to his at the hospital. In fact he and Paisley had played several games of chess together. It was from Paisley that Archibald had learned about these nightly patrols the navy had instituted in an effort to contain the epidemic.

If Archibald was very lucky then whoever was in charge of this unseen guard boat would have heard of Paisley, and might even know that Paisley had ended up in the hospital.

The best deceptions are founded on misconception and convincing detail.

Archibald cleared his throat and adopted a conciliatory tone. 'No need for alarm, I assure you. This is the *Marie Spindler*. We are here to make sure you are doing your duty. Any trouble tonight?'

'Stop and be boarded!' said the angry voice in the dark.

Archibald made no immediate reply. He had noticed that that the challenging voice *sounded further away.*

The schooner had managed to slip past the guard boat in the dark!

Archibald waited a few more minutes before continuing to act the part of a naval officer making a surprise inspection. 'As you were! Carry on! You are following procedures. But try to do something about those rowlocks. I mean it. That's an order!'

There was a pause.

'Aye aye, sir,' said the voice in the dark, sounding *much* further way now.

Young Tommy stroked his mouse, his eyes wide.

Archibald put a finger to his lips to remind the lad not to say a word.

The cracky grinned back. He gave Archibald a sly nod. This was *fun.*

A moment later *Marie Spindler* caught the wind.

She heeled in the offshore breeze and began to make a pleasing lapping sound under her bowsprit. She rounded the mole and headed south across the Bay of Rosia, racing through the dark to round Europa Point to make escape from Gibraltar before anybody sighted her.

Archibald's heart was still racing. What a close call! But his ruse had worked. He was on his way home. He really might see his wife after all these years. The Atlantic was one thousand seven hundred and seventy miles wide. The crossing would take weeks, and be fraught with danger, particularly at this time of the year. But with luck he might see his dear wife again.

It has been so long! How I miss you! How I yearn for you! What you are doing right now I wonder, Admiral Wentworth?

11

CHAPTER

ARCHIBALD'S WIFE, ADMIRAL WENTWORTH, had just
woken from a deep sleep.

Gunfire!

She sat up in bed.

She knew those guns. They were *her* guns.

Signal Hill was firing a salute!

She sighed and leaned back on her pillow.

She knew what that meant.

Her term as acting Governor and Commander-in-Chief of
the Newfoundland Station was ending. For years she had served
as a stand-in for James Gambier, after that statesman had left
the colony in haste to serve the new Pitt government as Lord
Commissioner of the Admiralty. Now Gambier's replacement was
arriving, none other than the celebrated Sir Erasmus Gower, the
very officer who had prevented the mutineers at the Spithead and
the Nore from going up the river to London. She had followed
Gower's career closely after that. Following long years of service in
China, the West Indies and the Falkland Islands, Gower had risen
to the rank of Rear-Admiral of the White. She looked forward to

meeting the man. Gower would take over the Station, and perhaps, if she was lucky, she might hear from Gower's own lips the very latest news from London. There might even be word of her children, James and Corrie Harriman, both of whom were serving naval officers. Had James and Corrie survived that huge battle off Cape Trafalgar? Would Gower know if they had?

She sighed. News took *weeks* to reach her out here at the naval station in St. John's.

What of her husband Archibald? The very last she had heard of him, Archibald had been serving alongside James and Corrie in the *Victory*. She had said prayers for all three of them, and now, this morning, she had better brace herself for news. That news might not be good. Trafalgar had taken many lives.

She looked in her long mirror. For this hand-over at the King's Wharf she must look every inch a male commanding officer. Gambier might or might not know her true gender. Either way, appearances had to be kept up, for this naval station had played a vital part in protecting the fishery on and about the Grand Banks. The cod fishery was huge, and extremely profitable for Britain. Both the French and the Americans had their eyes on the Grand Banks. No wonder Britain was sending Gower here! He would be a strong hand at the helm.

She strode out of Admiralty House, her ceremonial sword gleaming in the sun. The grand carriage conveyed her down the steep hillside to the dockside. This was the last time she would be allowed to commandeer the splendid Admiralty coach with its four fine white mares. She was going to miss those mares.

On her arrival at the wharf, in obedience to her own orders, the Royal Marine Bandsmen were drawn up, and busy playing airs.

She shaded her eyes from the sun and looked out across the water. She watched as the frigate *Shannon*, captained by Philip Broke if her memory served her right, proceeded through the Narrows and headed towards the dock taking full advantage of the mild south-westerly morning breeze. You could tell a lot about a captain by watching the way he handled his vessel in confined waters. Captain Broke seemed to know what he was about.

The waters of the harbour were thick with cod today!

The eagles on Pancake Island were having themselves a feast.

Perfect weather for our change of command.

The *Shannon* slid alongside the dock. Her men and women leaped ashore. They made fast the mooring cables to bollards. A gangway was lowered. Gambier and his people were waiting on the deck, dressed in their ceremonials. Gambier was a handsome-looking fellow.

It was time for music.

She caught the eye of the bandleader, and nodded.

Cymbals, fife and drums crashed out a noble welcome to the Rear-Admiral and new commanding officer. She recognized the popular air *Roll on, ye Billows of the Surgy Main!*

The Seaman thus, long tossed by stormy seas
Worn out with toil, and sinking with disease
With looks of rapture eyes the black'ning land
Forgets the past, and smiles at present pain
Feels a new vigour thrill through ev'ry vein
And leaps exulting on the welcome strand!

To the sound of this romantic refrain, her replacement stepped ashore, his hand to his hat brim.

The two admirals exchanged salutes.

They shook hands.

'Welcome to the Newfoundland Station, Sir Erasmus. Your reputation precedes you.'

'I'm pleased to be here, Admiral Wentworth. Allow me to introduce my officers.'

An hour of formalities passed before the two admirals were free to sit down together in the relative privacy of the governor's study in the official residence, to catch up with the latest gossip from at home and abroad.

She cleared her throat and looked keenly at Gower. 'I understand the recent battle off Cape Trafalgar was a success?'

'Prodigious. Eight French and nine Spanish ships captured. The *Achille* destroyed. Many more ships wrecked in the storm that followed. Napoleon's hope of invading England has been dashed.'

'I had family serving in the *Victory*.'

'Indeed. I made inquiries before I left England. I have mixed news for you,' said Gower carefully.

She caught her breath. Her mind raced.

'You imply that one or more of my family…?'

Gower frowned and continued. 'I am told that Captain Sir Corrie Harriman and Captain James Harriman survived the battle. I believe Corrie has been asked to take the Victory back to Chatham for refitting, while James has been given the responsibility of shepherding the annual by-boats here to Newfoundland for the summer's fishing. All the Admiralty could tell me about Lieutenant Archibald Harriman is that he is presently unaccounted for. Have you by any chance heard from him?'

'I have not.' Did Gower know she was a woman? He was speaking very carefully. It was hard to tell whether he knew or not.

She swallowed.

No word from Archibald.

She had not heard a word from her husband in the last six months. Was he dead?'

Gower held up his hand as if reading her mind. 'He may be among the wounded. Not all of the hospital sick lists are in.'

Her thoughts raced.

Gower is doing his best to be kind, but I know what he thinks. Archibald is no more. The chances are I shall never see Archibald again. He and I shall never again share a bed. I feel weak in my knees, but I must take care not show my weakness. People die in wars, but did it have to be the father of my children? I feel empty.

'Thank you for bringing me news of my family.'

'I wish the news were better.'

'How about your own people? Do you have family, Sir Erasmus?'

'I have lost several dear friends, but I have no family. My life has been devoted to representing Britain abroad.'

She pulled herself together. 'Napoleon's staff will surely remind him that our by-boats from the west of England will be bringing fisherfolk here for the season's fishing.'

Sir Erasmus Gower strode over to the chart mounted in a frame upon the wall. 'The Southern Shore is vulnerable?'

'The Bay of Plaisance is clear of ice. Unusual for this time of year. We have reoccupied Saint Pierre and Miquelon. A well-armed French squadron could take back both islands and sink all of the fishing boats there. It has been done before.'

'Your advice, Admiral Wentworth?'

'I would not waste our time and resources on Saint Pierre. I think Napoleon will order his squadron out into the Atlantic. With what instructions, I cannot imagine.'

'The cod fishery is vital to English trade.'

'Indeed. We sell salt fish at home and abroad in prodigious quantities.'

Gower leaned forward to peer more closely at the chart.

'A French squadron could show up here, in the Tail of the Grand Banks,' he suggested, tapping with his forefinger the region where the deep ocean began. 'We had better patrol the waters between the Whale Bank and the Southeast Shoal. Is the *Invulnerable* ready for service?'

'She is.'

'Very well then. Make her ready for sea. I shall lend you the *Shannon*. Captain Broke will need to restock with powder and shot. We saw some action on our way here.'

'Communications?'

'Better take half a dozen reliable pigeons with you, and let me know the moment you spot the French. I shall send whatever reinforcements I can spare.'

'Thank you, Governor. I think you'll find the staff here at the Residence efficient and trustworthy. There has been no further trouble with our local people since we hanged Farrell and Power for the murder of Lieutenant Lawry.'

'Yes, I read about that in the Chronicle,' said Gower, straightening his back. He strode to the window and gazed thoughtfully down at the shipping crowding the harbour. 'Good luck, Admiral,' he said.

So she was dismissed. Just like that.

'Governor.'

She let herself out of what had been her own study until early that morning, but was now Gower's.

The change of command rankled.

She was not in a good mood.

She found Captain Broke waiting for her in the antechamber. He was a saturnine individual with a strong jaw. She looked him directly in the eye. 'We are to go on patrol together, the *Invulnerable* and the *Shannon*. How soon can we leave?'

'The Dockyard Quartermaster is reluctant to part with salt beef, Admiral, and the Armourer claims that he has no chain shot.'

'I'll speak to them. You'll have your supplies, if I have to hang both of them. How soon can we sail?'

'Noon tomorrow.'

'Fair enough. No shore leave.'

'Understood, admiral.'

'Signal the *Invulnerable*. Tell them to send a boat for me. While I'm waiting for the boat I shall see to your supplies.'

When Quartermaster McCarthy failed to answer her knock on his office door, she ordered Marine Sergeant Roberts to put his shoulder to the door and break it.

The door burst open with a splintering crash.

The hapless Quartermaster leaped to his feet. He had been imbibing behind his desk. 'Governor!' he cried, doing his best to hide his flask from sight.

'I'm not your Governor any more, McCarthy, as you would know if you had not been drinking. Fifty tons of salt beef. Best quality. Immediately. On the dock. The *Shannon*'s crew will roll the casks for you. No returns, and it had better be your best beef. I shall be eating it.'

'I'll have it seen to, admiral,' said the Quartermaster, relaxing back into his chair and eyeing his flask hopefully. For a moment he had feared that the admiral had found out about his short-changing of the suppliers.

'You'll do it yourself McCarthy and you'll do it now. If the casks are not on the dock in one hour, then you are dismissed. You'll be *out of a job*. Do I make myself perfectly clear, Mr. McCarthy?'

'Yes, admiral,' said the wretched fellow, staring at her hopelessly. He was dying for another swig.

'Mr. McCarthy, *why* are you still here?'

'Oh! You mean *me*, personally? Right *now*?' The Quartermaster's jaw dropped.

Admiral Wentworth pulled her silver pocket watch from her fob. 'Fifty-nine minutes before you are dismissed.'

Mr. McCarthy grabbed his hat from his hat-stand and ran out of the room.

'Now for the Armoury, Sergeant!'

The Sergeant escorted her to the door of Mr. Prentice, the station armourer, and flung the door open.

Mr. Prentice was discovered to be fast asleep at his post.

'Chain-shot, Mr. Prentice!' shouted Admiral Wentworth in a voice. Loud enough to wake the Dead. 'Ten tons in the *Shannon*'s shot locker by sunset.'

The Armourer sat up with a start. 'Can't be done.'

'Mr. Prentice, you will recall I had three tiers of chain-shot delivered to you last April. Surely you have not forgotten.'

Mr. Prentice shrugged his shoulders. 'Maybe next week, or the week after.'

'Marine-Sergeant Roberts will lend you his marines to shift the shot, won't you, Marine-Sergeant?'

'Yes, admiral.'

'Better show the sergeant where you keep our chain-shot, Mr. Prentice.'

Mr. Prentice gazed at her in blank-faced astonishment. Everybody knew she was not a real man.

'The Marine-Sergeant grows impatient, Mr. Prentice. A few minutes ago the Marine-Sergeant stove in the door to the Quartermaster's office. He is presently eyeing your walnut desk with its handsome ivory inlay.'

Prentice took one look at the Marine-Sergeant, grabbed his keys from a nail on the wall, and dashed past them. 'This way,' he cried, cursing silently. The nerve of the woman!

Marine-Sergeant Roberts glanced inquiringly at his admiral. She gave him a nod.

Marine-Sergeant Roberts would see to it that Captain Broke received by sundown all the supplies that were needed to refurbish the *Shannon*.

She would be sleeping in a different bed tonight.

She was woken early by her pigeon handler.

'So sorry to bother you so early, admiral.'

She rubbed the sleep from her eyes. 'Come in, Winifred. I have fewer responsibilities now that Sir Erasmus has taken over. You have something for me?'

'Adarna showed up in our dovecot overnight. When I went to feed the birds this morning, there was Adarna looking as pleased as Punch with herself.'

'Wasn't that the bird we lent to Corrie's Admiralty agent, Mrs. Keeper?'

'Yes, m'am. That's the one. She has a black tail feather.'

The Admiral whistled. 'She has made a long flight. The message?'

'It is addressed to you, and marked Private and Confidential.'

The admiral's heart missed a beat. She held out her hand. 'Thank you very much, Winifred. You may go now. Keep up the good work! Your birds will be the undoing of Napoleon.'

'I hope they make a difference, admiral,' said the handler, looking pleased with herself as she left, closing the bedroom door behind her.

For a moment, Corrie's mother looked at the tiny scrolled up message lying in her palm.

There had been no word of her husband since the battle.

This message might well be from the Admiralty confirming his death.

She took a deep breath.

She unwound the scroll with trembling fingers.

The message was not about her husband at all.

She read the message carefully and then reread it.

Napoleon was sending out from Brest a French squadron of five ships of the line, two frigates and a corvettes, under Contre-Amiral Leisségues. Leisségues's flagship was the 120-gun *Impérial*. He had with him the *Alexandre* (80 guns) the *Brave* (74 guns) the *Diomède* (74 guns) and the *Jupiter* (74 guns). This force was heading out into the Atlantic. Her spy reported that the decks of the flagship were seen to be crowded with *uniformed troops*.

This was important news. Perhaps it would be as well if she had this particular message relayed to the Governor *after* her departure.

Napoleon meant to have revenge on the British for his defeat off Cape Trafalgar. Where was this French squadron headed with so many soldiers? Not the Grand Banks. Oh, no! Somewhere in the Carib Sea, almost certainly. The French had possessions on those islands that were part of their overseas empire. The French had immensely profitable sugar plantations, manned by hundreds of slaves.

Wherever the French squadron is bound, I must stir my stumps and find a way to confront that French squadron. I won't pass this message on to Gower. He might try to prevent me from leaving. I'll write a note for Gower and place it somewhere where he is sure to find it after *I have sailed in the* Invulnerable *in the company of the* Shannon. *I met Rear-Admiral Leisségues once at a ball and we chatted. He is a dangerous and far-sighted opponent. I had better find this French squadron of his, and sink it, or all that Britain has just gained by her victory off Cape Trafalgar will be at hazard. Leisségues must be taking his thousand troops somewhere...*

12

CHAPTER

AMIRAL CORENTIN URBAIN LEISSÉGUES listened with growing impatience to the ravings of Captain Bigot who had been appointed to command his flagship the *Impérial* and deliver the troops he was ferrying from France to Santo Domingo. Bigot seemed to hold a dim view of the people of the Islands. Leisségues sighed. The decks of his flagship were crowded with noisy, chattering soldiers, many of whom were Islanders looking forward seeing their homeland again after years of training and fighting overseas.

The sooner he was rid of all these cursed landsmen, the better it would be for the morale of his squadron. If only he could rid himself of this importunate officer Bigot. There was something about this fellow that simply did not add up. So far as he, Admiral Leisségues was concerned, Captain Bigot was a tiresome, uneducated fellow. Irksome, if the truth be told. The admiral sighed. Day after day he had had to put up with Bigot's tirades. He had to wonder if the man was even sane? His methods of imposing discipline were *extremely* questionable.

'*Mon dieu!*' the infuriating fool of a captain was shouting in his face. 'What is it that you do not understand, admiral? All over the world these Islanders they are dangerous. You know this is true. Why, our emperor himself he has said this!'

Leisségues drew a silk kerchief from his fob and dabbed his cheek to remove the idiot's spittle from his cheek. 'Let us try to be calm, captain,' he said without raising his voice. It was important to adopt a moderate tone when speaking to an imbecile. He was not sure whom he found the most intolerable, this Captain Bigot or these cursed soldiers cluttering up his decks. The mad captain had to be placated and reminded of his manners.

'These punishment parades of yours have to stop, Captain Bigot. We simply cannot murder our own people.'

'People?' shouted the upstart officer .'You call these ignorant Islanders people? They are *animals*, admiral. They dance and sing without permission! They misbehave! You *know* we have to put them down. Why, I have seen you punish your own mariners.'

'I do not throw my mariners over the side to drown. So allow me to refresh your memory, captain. These are our *troops*. Many will die when we reach the islands, probably of yellow fever. I have served in the *Caraïbes* myself, you know. I have very considerable experience of fighting here in the Islands.'

The crazy captain was not in the mood to listen to reason. 'Look at my face!' the pitiful excise for a disciplinarian cried. Can you not see it there in my cheeks, admiral? The *jaunice*?'

The admiral took a deep breath. 'Perhaps your *jaunice* explains your extraordinary tantrums. A few minutes ago I was appalled to hear from one of my officers that you had with your own hands tied old flour sacks around the necks of six of our own soldiers and then you yourself with your own hands had pushed those six perfectly healthy soldiers pushed over the side to drown. Please tell me this isn't true? Please tell me you have not just drowned six of the very men you are going to need to regain control of our colony of Santo Domingo? Surely I do not have to remind you that we embarked a thousand soldiers? How many of those soldiers will be left to serve us if you continue to slaughter them in this arbitrary fashion?

Captain Bigot grew red in the face. He pounded his palm with his fist. 'There is nothing arbitrary about my methods, admiral. These scum are Islanders pretending to be soldiers! They wear our *uniform*. That in itself it makes my skin crawl. When we reach Santo Domingo I plan to kill all the Islanders of the mountains, yes, every last man and woman. I intend to spare only children under twelve years of age. After that I shall proceed to kill *half of the Islanders living in the plains*. Rest assured, admiral, we shall not leave alive a *single* Islander in the colony who has worn an epaulette. That much I have *promised* the Emperor in this my campaign to win back the island for France. This is a war of extermination. Trust me. I know what I am doing.'

'I do not trust you, sir. I find your actions reprehensible, whatever you may have promised our emperor. You are *not* to kill any more of your own soldiers while on board *my* ship and your men are under *my* protection. I hope this is understood?'

'*Sacrebleu!* My soul is withered.'

'I doubt very much that you have a soul, sir. So let me be blunt. My officers will *arrest* you if you murder any more of our soldiers.'

The lunatic drew himself up to his full height, which was not very great, and glared up at this pitiful admiral who dared to confront him. 'Bah!' he said. 'You know *nothing* of the art of war.'

The Admiral put a rasp into his voice. 'Say that to the British in Guadeloupe. You may remember that I retook the island from them. I did *not* win back that island by slaughtering all the native people.'

Captain Bigot lowered his voice to a hoarse whisper. 'They are not people. In your heart, you know this.'

The Admiral stood his ground. 'They look like people to me. You had better start treating them like people or I shall have a bag of flour tied around *your* neck.'

'*Mon dieu!* You threaten a fellow officer?'

'I'm not even convinced that you *are* a fellow officer. Lieutenant Papillon tells me he was present on the day when our late lamented General Charles Leclerc ordered the execution of one thousand Islander soldiers dressed in French military uniforms. He says that the late general tied sacks of flour around the necks of his own soldiers and pushed them into the sea to drown. Lieutenant Papillon swears that General Leclerc died of yellow fever four weeks later. Papillon attended Leclerc's funeral. So who do you think you are, Captain Bigot? Wait! My *lieutenant de vaisseau* requires my attention. Yes, Lieutenant Alarie? You are worried about the clouds massing on the horizon?'

The lieutenant saluted and then made his report. 'The water in the baromètre Liegèois, she is rising. We have reset the device twice, with the same result, my admiral.'

'A storm is coming.'

'A big one.'

'I understand. Clear the decks! Captain Bigot, have all our soldiers, and I mean all of them, ushered down into the hold. The soldiers are to be told to lie down flat. They are *not* to load their weapons. You may tell them that we shall call on them when we need them.'

'*Bien entendu,* my admiral,' said Captain Bigot, his eyes lighting up with unholy glee. 'I shall treat them like the dogs they are. I shall whip them into obedience.'

There came an excited shout from the masthead. 'Strange sail! One of our frigates, captain. She is the *Belle Poule,* and that one she is racing towards us under full sail. Holà! I see many other smaller vessels riding the waves. *Mon amiral!* I believe we have discovered a *convoi de navires!*'

'A convoy!' Leisségues's face lit up. 'Praise be to God! We have discovered the British fishing fleet!' He rubbed his hands together with glee. 'The moment we have the soldiers stowed away, our guns are to be loaded and run out. Topsails and foresail. Fighting trim, Captain Bigot.'

'*Bien sûr,*' said Captain Julien-Gabriel Bigot, lashing out at a passing Islander with his rawhide whip.

Bigot was proud of his ship and his crew. He took a moment to gaze at the *Belle Poule* through his far-seeing-glass. The *Belle Poule* had been captured by the British many years ago. She was flying the flag of revolutionary France today, but he knew that was a ruse. He wondered whether the British captain of the *Belle Poule* had any idea what he faced. Bah! The British were so over-confident. Their arrogance would be their undoing. He found it very annoying that his Islander-loving admiral kept anticipating his commands. If only there were some polite way to remind the admiral that it was he, Julien-Gabriel Bigot, and not the admiral, who was in charge of the *Impérial,* and that it was he, Julien-Gabriel Bigot and his hard-working crew who were putting up with all these vomiting unruly Islanders presently being led below and told to lie down flat amid the *Impérial*'s 200 tons of iron ballast and 150 tons of shingle. It was he and his crew who would have to have that ballast spread out on some dockside one day and hosed down. The Islanders they were animals. General Charles Leclerc had been right to drown a thousand of them. If he had his way, he, Bigot, would drown all one thousand of them, not just the six he had pushed over the side himself minutes ago.

Admiral Leisségues cleared his throat. 'Signal the *Alexandre*, the *Brave*, the *Diomède*, and the *Jupiter*. Tell them to engage the enemy. We shall recapture this *Belle Poule* from the English. She will make a useful addition to our squadron.'

'Yes, my admiral.'

Signal flags broke out.

There was another shout from the masthead. 'Sir! The *Belle Poule* is raising the Black Ball! She has the plague!' squeaked a young officer.

Leisségues raised his voice to reply. 'I doubt that, *aspirant*. You forget that the British are not be trusted. They are Huguenots, they are without morals. They are trying to frighten us, but we shall not be not frightened. We have 120 guns. The Belle Poule has 40.'

'Boarding party away!' said Captain Bigot.

'Good.' The admiral reached for his speaking trumpet to instruct the officer in charge of the boarders. 'Aspirant Cocault! Spare the life of the British captain. Confiscate his sword and bring him to me in irons. I should like a word or two with him.'

'Yes, my admiral,' replied Cocault, saluting his admiral.

Admiral Leisségues turned to the loathsome Bigot. 'The British captain may have valuable information regarding British intentions. I need intelligence. The British have their cursed pigeons carrying messages for them.'

'The *Belle Poule* is not alone, admiral,' replied Bigot, adjusting his far-seeing glass

'What do you mean?'

'A second British vessel is closing fast. Another frigate. Admiral, this is strange. I can see *six of our own soldiers* standing on the deck of the second British vessel.'

'Surely you are mistaken?'

'No, my admiral. I see them clearly. I see six of our own uniformed soldiers standing right there on the enemy's Quarter Deck. All six are Islanders. They are talking to the British captain.'

Admiral Leisségues crossed himself. 'Your drowned soldiers have come back from the dead to haunt us. I feel weak at the knees. I *warned* you, did I not?'

13

CHAPTER

BILLY BROWN sang out from the maintop, and pointed ahead.

Corrie extended her telescope to have a look.

'They may be seals. Want to have a look at them, Nathaniel?'

Her youngster was learning to use a telescope.

She helped him point the glass in the right direction.

'Mama, why is one of the seals waving?'

Corrie snatched the telescope back for a second look. 'Man overboard!' she shouted. 'Helm! Bring us up into the wind! Galley away!'

The deck canted as the *Swift* came to sudden halt on the very crest of a wave, brought up all standing by her order. Corrie grabbed Nathaniel by one arm to steady the youngster. 'Back and fill! Keep her so!' she ordered. 'Can you keep us in irons, Mackenzie?'

The helmswoman nodded. It was no easy matter to keep a vessel as large as the *Swift* in irons in weather as threatening as this. Canvas clapped and snapped. Spray flew up into the air. Mackenzie shifted her wad of tobacco from one cheek to the other and took a quick look at the ship's pennant streaming from the masthead. There was a storm in the offing. Enemy vessels were in sight. This was a dangerous moment.

'Ease the galley down! Steady as she goes!' ordered Lieutenant Keeper. The galley crew had to be quick. There seemed to be *several seals* rising and falling on the waves as the galley drew closer. Wait a minute! They were not seals, They were *sacks of flour*. They were closing with the enemy squadron. Some French cook must have thrown empty sacks over the side.

'Row like the dickens!'

The rescue crew put their backs into it.

Lieutenant Keeper was pleased with the way the galley handled the swells. Long hours of rowing practice had paid off. His rowers knew what they were about. Their timing was good. But were there lives to be saved? Or was this merely a wild goose chase?

They had manned and rowed the galley over and over again in drills, but on this occasion they had a mission.

Would they be in time? Had that really been a drowning man that the captain said she had glimpsed? Their galley had to be the fastest craft afloat! If anything could save men from drowning, it was this speedy galley of theirs.

From her Quarter Deck, Corrie watched the recue bid with a keen eye. She and young Nathaniel had glimpsed a wildly thrashing human arm. *Someone* was in trouble. But who? And why? And would her galley arrive in time?

Very soon she would have to give the command to send the *Swift* racing to close with Leisségues's squadron in the teeth of what looked very much like a bad storm. Evidently the French had suffered storm damage. The *Alexandre* had lost a mizzen mast, and the *Brave* was listing to port. Corrie was hardly surprised. Having been cooped up in Brest by the Royal Navy blockade for years and years, the French navy were sorely out of practice when it came to seamanship. Corrie was sure that the crew of the *Brave* were hard at work with shovels down in their hold shifting tons of iron ballast from one side of the ship to the other in a concerted effort to bring their warship back on an even keel. One strong gust of wind could capsize the *Brave*. The clouds massing on the horizon told her that a strong gust or two might be coming? But wait! She stiffened. She was forestalled! There was *another sail* closing with the French. That would be her brother in the *Belle Poule*, acting like the brave fool he was. And she had just launched her galley, and was losing vital minutes attempting a rescue. How frustrating!

'Mamma, what are the people in the boat doing? Are they going to talk to the seals?'

'They may not be seals, Nat. They may be people. If they are people, then the men in the boat will save try to them.'

'What if they are seals?' asked Nathaniel.

'If they are seals, then the men in the boat will leave them be. Seals can swim.'

Nathaniel ran to the rail to get a better view. 'They are *not* seals,' he said, disappointed. He wanted seals. 'They are just people.'

'I believe you are right, Nat,' said Corrie, adjusting her lens once more. 'Yes, indeed they *are* people. But they are not *our* people. They are wearing French uniforms. They are soldiers. Six of them.'

Minutes later the galley dashed back to the ship with six coughing and spluttering enemy soldiers. The poor half-drowned wretches were helped aboard the *Swift*.

The galley was swung back on board and stowed on the gun deck.

Corrie gave the order for the *Swift* to resume her course. It was time to engage the French squadron.

Lieutenant Keeper hurried aft to make his report, accompanied by the six rescued French soldiers. He held up a sodden flour bag. 'French soldiers. All Islanders. They had these sacks tied round their necks. Somebody in the French squadron must have pushed them over the side to drown. The fellow who waved at us is talking up a storm about something. I can't understand a word the fellow is saying.'

Corrie raised her voice. 'Billy Brown to the Quarter Deck!'

Billy Brown was an Islander. Perhaps Billy Brown could translate what these half-drowned enemy soldiers had to say?

Billy slid down the mainstay, eager to chat with the rescued Islanders.

One of the Islanders stared at Billy, wild-eyed.

'Sa ki non'w?'

'Billy Brown,' she replied. 'Bon jou.'

'Mwen vlé yon bwè.'

'He says he is thirsty, captain.'

Corrie turned to her young son. 'Fetch this French soldier a mug of fresh water from the tub, Nat. You know where the tub is.'

Nathaniel raced off barefoot to fetch the man who was not a seal a mug of water from the huge barrel by the foot of the middle of the three big tall wooden things that went way up into the air.

As he raced along the deck, dodging this way and that between the big people, and repeated over and over in his mind his mother's words about *fetching the water*. He had to remember what he was supposed to be doing. He had to keep on remembering.

Fetch this French soldier a mug of fresh water from the tub, Nat.

Nathaniel found it easy to be distracted. He had to keep reminding himself to *fetch fresh water from the tub, in a mug*. He knew what fresh water was. He knew there was fresh water for the asking in the big round thing. He *thought* he knew what a mug was. Mugs were those things you could dip into the water when you wanted to have a drink? Mugs hung from pegs. He knew that much.

But how did you get a mug off a peg? He wasn't sure.

He slid to a halt in front of the peg board.

He looked up, up, up.

Yes, he could see mugs way up there, swinging this way and that with the movement of the ship. In a ship, everything moved all the time. The mugs were made of wood. The mugs were beyond his reach. He would have to jump up to grab one.

He took a deep breath.

He bent at the knees.

He jumped.

The ends of his fingers touched a mug! He was almost there!

He tried again. This time he jumped a little higher and hit the mug. The mug swung wildly.

But the mug did *not* come off its peg.

He became angry.

Stupid mug!

He went red in the face.

A deep voice in his ear said 'Now, little captain. How about I give you a hoist?'

Nathaniel knew that voice. That was the voice of the big man in the red coat who was in charge of the ship's band.

He felt two huge hands take hold of him under his armpits.

His feet left the ground.

He was up in the air!

Now the swinging mugs were within his reach. He grabbed one mug and it came right off its peg.

'Now for the water,' said the deep voice in his ear. 'Help yourself, little sir.'

The world swung around and Nathaniel found himself looking down into water slopping back and forth *inside a huge barrel*.

'Dip your mug into the middle of the cask,' said the helpful marine sergeant. 'Best to steer clear of them there green mucky-ducky around the sides of the cask.'

Nathaniel's mouth hung open. The water cask was alive! There were swimming things!

He did as he was told.

He lowered the mug into the middle of the water.

He frowned.

This was *very odd*.

He had to *push* the mug down into the water.

The water *pushed back*, trying to stop him!

'Woo!' he said.

'Deeper,' said the man from the band helpfully.

Nathaniel pushed the mug deeper.

Brrr! The water felt cold.

It went up to his elbows.

He shivered.

He went on pushing the mug down.

Nothing happened.

He frowned.

He took a deep breath.

He bit his lip.

He could *do* this.

He forced the mug down some more…

Suddenly water flowed over the rim of the mug and filled it. That was exciting! He didn't have to push down any more.

He tried lifting the mug up.

The mug felt heavy now.

Very heavy!

He had to hold onto the heavy mug tightly with both hands.

'Let me down!' he said to the big person in the red coat.

The bandsman lowered Nathaniel back down to the deck. As Nathaniel's bare feet took his weight, the big hands let go of him.

Phew! He was on his own again. He was free.

He was holding a heavy mug of water.

What was he supposed to do with this mug of water?

He had forgotten.

He was so busy trying to remember what to do next that he quite forgot to thank the man in the red coat with the deep voice.

Then it came to him. He remembered.

Fetch this French soldier a mug of fresh water from the tub, Nat.

That was what his mother had told him.

That was what he had to do next.

He walked carefully back towards where his mother was.

It was taking too long?

He broke into a run.

Uh-oh!

Some of the water slopped out of the mug.

He slowed down.

That was safer.

Fresh water was precious.

He had to get this fresh water all the way back to the man who was not a seal.

He must *not* spill any more of the fresh water.

He was getting there.

He could hear his mother's voice talking to Billy.

Nathaniel knew Billy.

'Billy, would you please ask our visitor who it was who ordered the bag of flour tied around his neck and had him pushed him over the side of his ship?'

The stranger told Billy his story. He gestured wildly with his hands. He made faces to explain how it felt to be struggling for air and thrashing about in the sea. He spoke a name familiar to Corrie.

'Wait. Billy. Did he say…?'

'Captain Bigot,' said Billy. 'He says Captain Bigot gave order. Captain, I need to talk to you.'

'Later, Billy. What ship is our rescued man from? Ask him!'

'He says he is from the *Impérial*. The French flagship.'

Corrie nodded.

That made sense. The *Impérial* must be headed for Santo Domingo, probably bringing reinforcements for the French garrison there.

There was a flash of lightning.

The other British frigate, her brother's *Belle Poule,* was about to engage the enemy flagship. The *Belle Poule* was hugely out-gunned.

'What else does our half-drowned French soldier have to tell us?' asked Corrie, anxious to learn all she could about her enemy.

'He *say* he not know why the captain had him pushed into sea to drown. He is lying, captain.'

Corrie stared at Billy, appalled. 'Are you telling me that you know why Captain Bigot pushed these fellows over the side to drown? Is that what you are telling me, Billy?'

Billy set her mouth in a hard line. She looked Corrie straight in the eye. She made no reply.

Her silence was worth a thousand words.

Corrie turned to Lieutenant Keeper. 'Lieutenant, do you understand what Billy is *not* telling us?'

'I do so, sir, and I'm... appalled, captain. Absolutely appalled.'

Corrie clenched her fists. 'So am I. Our six rescued soldiers are to be treated respectfully. They are *not* be made fun of. They are *not* be treated as prisoners. I wish to make them *our friends*. Ask each one of them what their duties in the Grand Armée.'

The question brought all six half-drowned soldiers to life. They gabbled in their native tongue.

'They are bandsmen. Captain. They play instruments. This big fellow here plays the bugle.'

Corrie's brain raced. That might be useful. 'Ask him if he can play the Charge and the Retreat?'

'He says yes, he can play both, and the Reveille. Here comes Nathaniel.'

Nathaniel was walking gingerly. He was carrying the heavy wooden mug tightly between his small hands, trying not to spill any more than he had already. He went straight up to the man who was not a seal and held out the mug.

'Water,' he said helpfully.

The half-drowned enemy soldier stared at the child for moment, and then reached out with trembling hands, took hold of the mug, and drained it in a single swallow.

'*Gracias*,' he said.

Nathaniel's eyes widened. He had never seen anybody drink a mug of water so fast.

His face lit up in a smile.

When the stranger saw Nathaniel smile, he put the empty mug on the deck and pretended the mug was an pig. 'Oink!' he said. "Oink! Oink!' He made the mug run this way and that like a pig.

Nathaniel laughed. He stared enthralled at the mug that had become a pig.

Then the stranger returned the mug to Nathaniel.

Nathaniel looked at his mother as if to say: 'Did you see that, mother? The mug was a pig!'

Corrie rewarded her boy with a smile.

'Take the mug back to the water barrel,' she said. 'Fetch more water.'

Her child ran off to do so.

Corrie watched him go.

Nathaniel is beginning to understand the workings of a frigate. Perhaps one day he shall have a frigate of his own to look after. I hope Nathaniel never has to face an enemy as prejudiced and cruel as this French Captain Bigot who pushes his own soldiers overboard to drown!

She returned her gaze to the rescued man who knew how to play with her child, and, more importantly from her point of view, who knew how to play the *bugle*.

'Sergeant Deering! Fetch this man a bugle! Quickly!'

The stranger regarded her very seriously. His fate was in her hands. Perhaps he was expecting her to throw him back into the sea.

They had to win over this bugle player.

They were fast running out of time.

Sergeant Deering returned with a bugle.

'Give the bugle to this rescued man. Let's see what he can do with it. Billy, ask him to sound the 'Charge.'

The half-drowned bandsman seized the bugle eagerly, and the ship resounded with an exhilarating call to action.

'Good. Now ask him to play the Retreat.'

The haunting, plaintive sound to be heard when the evening colours were being hauled down resounded through the *Swift*, and inquisitive heads appeared in hatchways.

'A private word, captain?' asked Billy daringly.

'Step into my cabin.'

She led Billy into the relative privacy of her own quarters.

'Yes?' she asked shortly. She had a battle to fight. This had better be important.

Billy made a sign of warding. 'No good kill Dutty Duppy with sword. Dutty Duppy come *back*.'

Corrie stared at Billy in amazement. 'You are talking about the French captain who pushes his own soldiers over the side to drown? How *do* you kill a Dutty Duppy, Billy?'

'Give dat Dutty Duppy back own medicine. Whatever bad things that Dutty Duppy did, you do same bad things to him. Then you blow that Dutty Duppy away, like this...' Billy pursed her lips and blew softly into her cupped palms as if blowing away a speck of dust.'

There came a loud knock on the cabin door.

'Captain! The other British frigate is making a run for the *Impérial*. She has just raised a flag with a black ball on it. She is the *Belle Poule*. One of the hands recognized her fore topsail. Your brother's command.'

Corrie stiffened.

Her brother was charging into action without thinking first.

A *situation* was developing.

The wind was gusting.

The sky was darkening.

'Thanks for the advice, Billy. I have to go back up on deck.'

Up in the open air again, Corrie stood with her feet wide apart, her uniform jacket flapping madly as the *Swift* clawed her way towards the French, close-reefed, her standing rigging singing. Through the driving rain, she caught a glimpse of Leisségue's flagship, the 120-gun *Impérial*. But where had the *other* ships of the French squadron got to? The *Alexandre* and the *Brave*?

Her brother James's frigate, the *Belle Poule*, was closing fast with the enemy flagship.

She loved her brother, but he was a pain in the neck.

She was the senior officer. Properly speaking, it was up to *her* to order an attack on the French if such an attack were warranted. But she knew her brother would pay no attention to any signals she sent him, not at this juncture. James was committed. He was racing in to attack the French. She had just learned from the rescued half-drowned soldiers that the *Impérial* was headed for the French colony at Santo Domingo. Her brother might not be aware that he was attacking a ship-of-the line *crammed with troops*. It was her duty, as well as his, to prevent the French soldiers from being landed. She and her brother were hopelessly outnumbered and facing no less than *five* enemy ships: the *Impérial* of 120 guns, the *Alexandre* of 80 guns, and three 74s, the *Brave*, the *Diomède*, and the *Jupiter*. In addition there had to be other smaller warships in the offing. To attack so many powerful enemy vessels with two frail frigates was absurd, but it was the duty of every commanding officer to close with the enemy. Nelson had taught her that at Copenhagen.

What would Nelson do if he were in her shoes right now?

She knew *exactly* what he would do.

'Billy, I want the French bandsman to sound the Charge. Ask the man if he is willing to accompany our boarding party.'

There was a rapid exchange in the patois of the Islanders.

The rescued bandsmen doubled up with laughter.

Billy had them in fits.

'Well, Billy?'

'He can't wait to get their hands on Captain Bigot. Dis man say yes, he ready sound the Charge!'

The bugler gave a toot on his bugle.

He grinned at Corrie from ear to ear.

'That is a yes, captain.

'Mr. Hartnell, open the arms chest. Arm every man for boarding.'

Thunder crashed overhead.

Hailstones the size of walnuts came thundering down on the deck.

14

CHAPTER

'BRING US ALONGSIDE the *Belle Poule*! Lieutenant Keeper, look after my ship! Sergeant Deering! Sergeant Wilkes! Bayonets! You're with me!'

Corrie leaped aboard her brother's frigate.

The half-drowned enemy bandsman put the bugle to his mouth and sounded a tremendous Charge!

'Swifts with me!' Corrie shouted.

She raced across the deck of the *Belle Poule*. Her brother and his people were already clambering aboard the French flagship. She and her boarding party joined in the reckless attack shouting loudly. Corrie had to find this enemy captain who pushed his own soldiers overboard to drown, this Captain Bigot.

The bugler will know the man who tried to drown him.

Billy Brown shouted 'He know who!'

This did not bode well for Captain Bigot.

A second flash of lightning lit up the struggling crowd of men, women and children.

The six half-drowned French soldiers, still dressed in their sodden uniforms, dashed past Corrie and headed straight for the enemy Quarter Deck . One of them was carrying a flour sack!

Corrie grinned.

That did not bode *at all* well for Captain Bigot.

Corrie ran forward, delivering in passing a savage blow to the stomach of a female sailor who tried to prevent her.

She arrived out of breath to find the senior French navy and army officers with their backs to the mast, fending off British boarders from the *Belle Poule* and the *Swift*.

The bugler pointed out the enemy captain, Captain Bigot.

Bigot wore a stiff-necked embroidered collar, and a huge plumed hat. His cheeks were strangely sallow. Perhaps he was ill? Perhaps that helped explain his behavior?

'He is *already dead*, this Dutty Duppy,' Billy reminded her in a hoarse whisper.

Corrie curled her hand around the hilt of her sword and sprang forward to tackle Captain Bigot corps-à-corps.

A quick parry, a riposte, a counter attack.

The Dutty Duppy had her at a disadvantage.

Damn, but he was good! She was fighting a ghost.

Corrie was fighting a losing battle.

This is the man who drowns Islanders.

Footwork, footwork!

Sweat ran down Corrie's neck.

She ducked under the Frenchman's guard.

She pressed him hard.

But the fellow was too strong for her.

Captain Bigot looked at someone over Corrie's shoulder.

His jaw dropped.

What was this that was coming to pass?

Who was this waving an empty flour sack?

The flour sack was slid down over the general's head and tied firmly.

'This butu lacks broughtupsy,' said Billy.

Billy and the other Islanders carried Captain Bigot to the side of the ship.

They heaved the wicked murderer of bandsmen over the rail and into the sea.

Corrie heard a splash and a muffled yell of rage as Captain Bigot hit the sea.

'*En evant!*' he cried, his voice muffled by the sacking.

At this command, hundreds of angry French soldiers poured up the companionway of the *Impérial* determined to sweep the blasphemous British heathen off their decks.

Corrie blanched.

There were too many soldiers.

Her people were outnumbered.

She grabbed the grinning bugler's arm and shouted in his ear.

'*Sonner la retraite!*' she cried, and then pantomimed the act of sounding the bugle.

The first mournful bars of the Retreat sounded loud above the din of the battle. Had she left it too late?

'Swifts! Back to our ship!' she roared, and took a flying leap back down onto the deck of the *Belle Poule*, almost tripping over her own sword. She scrambled to regain her footing. Her people stopped sabotaging the *Impérial*'s halyards and stays — it would be hours before the French flagship would be able to sail again – and ran to join in the retreat.

Her brother James leaped down to join her. 'I didn't know you had a bugler!' he shouted.

'What happened to all those fishing boats you are supposed to be convoying?' Corrie wanted to know.

Her brother laughed. 'They have vanished over the horizon. I have lost an entire convoy!' Her reckless brother gave her a clap on the back. 'When shall we three meet again?'

Corrie was the senior officer. It was a reasonable question.

'English harbour. Report there to Admiral Cochrane,' she said in his ear. 'I have sent a prize to English Harbour for adjudication, a French guard ship. If you come across William Allen in English Harbour, please give him my respects. He is there to investigate slavery in our plantations. Try to help him if you can.'

'See you in English Harbour!' James whispered back, and a moment later brother and sister were parted by the rush of boarders returning to their respective ships just as the last sad notes of Retreat died away.

The crews of the *Belle Poule* and the *Swift* had left the deck of the French flagship, carrying wounded along with them.

It had been an orderly retreat.

Corrie was back on the deck of her own frigate.

The two British frigates parted company under cover of the storm.

Glancing back, Corrie saw Captain Bigot being hauled aboard one of the *Impérial*'s pinnaces. She saw a soldier cut the flour sack away from around Captain Bigot's neck. Was Bigot dead or alive? Corrie could not tell.

Huge waves churned up by the tropical storm made further fighting impossible. Rain pounded down out of the sky, hitting the sea so hard that it was deafening.

She cupped her hands around Billy's ear. 'Bare sticks!' she shouted.

Billy nodded and beckoned to her people, who raced for the ratlines and made their way out onto the yards to bind the canvas tightly to prevent it being torn from its gaskets.

The French squadron had vanished from sight.

So had her brother's ship.

Towering waves hauled the *Swift* up into the air, and slid her back down into a steep-sided valley of seawater.

Corrie grabbed hold of a stay and clung on for dear life.

The tempest lasted all through the night and for most of the next day.

When the storm abated, Corrie searched the horizon in vain for sign of other ships. There were none to be seen.

The *Swift* was left all alone in a wide blue sea.

So Corrie took a noon sight, spread out her chart of the Carib Sea on the floor of her cabin and set a course for English Harbour, home to the Leeward Islands Station that was the principal British naval base in this part of the world.

15

CHAPTER

AS CORRIE sailed into English Harbour, her glass revealed several familiar vessels at anchor in the outer reaches. There was her prize, the guard ship that Lieutenant Keeper had captured in the mouth of the Gironde. Corrie had ordered Lieutenant Partridge and William Allen to deliver her prize to this very naval station for adjudication by a Prize Court. By now, Allen would have made good on his promise to document the treatment of slaves in a British sugar plantation in this part of the world. On the other side of the harbour she spied her brother's frigate the *Belle Poule,* made fast to a wharf. She could see gaping holes on her starboard side where the French flagship's broadside had fired into her. It was a wonder her brother's frigate was still afloat. She took her hat off to her brother for bringing his battered craft safely to this safe haven for repairs.

More encouraging still was the sight of an entire British squadron lying at anchor further down the Roads. This had to be the squadron commanded by Sir John Thomas Duckworth, the squadron Anne had briefed Corrie about in confidence at Chatham.

Corrie knew several of Duckworth's warships. That must be the *Superb*, anchored beside the *Alexander*, the latter flying Cochrane's flag, and also, a little further down the bay, she spotted the *Northumberland*, the *Atlas*, the *Magicienne*, the *Spencer*, the *Agamemnon* and the *Donegal*. In addition there were several other ships of war unfamiliar to her. But there was something very familiar about that final ship-of-the-line just coming into view behind the *Agamemnon*. The sight of those masts and spars sent shivers up her spine. This was surely her mother's flagship, the *Invulnerable*.

What was her mother's flagship doing here in the Leeward Islands? What was her mother Admiral Wentworth doing here? The last Corrie had heard, her mother had been in charge of the St. John's naval station.

Corrie saw flags race up the mizzen halyard of the *Invulnerable*.

Mark Jater, her alert petty officer of signals, scribbled something on his slate. 'Signal from the *Invulnerable*, captain,' he reported. 'Our number. THE MARQUIS OF CARABAS.'

Corrie stiffened. That was her mother. No doubt about it. 'Reply NO NEWS OF THE OGRE.'

In making that sad reply, Corrie was beset with sorrow. Evidently her mother *was* here in English Harbour, and her mother anxious for news of her husband Archibald. Corrie brushed a tear from her eye. She did her best to pull herself together. She was captain. She must not let anyone aboard know that she was human and had family ties. It could be fatal for discipline to show her feelings. During the Battle off Cape Trafalgar, she had ordered her father to board a prize and to take command of that prize. She had not seen or heard from him since, and now, today, this covert exchange of signals between herself and her mother told her that her mother, too, had heard no word from Corrie's father.

That meant Archibald was dead for sure.

Missing in action.

That was really the only plausible explanation.

Corrie dis her best to thrust the emptiness she felt firmly to the back of her mind.

She had work to do.

She had arrived at last at the Leeward Islands Station, the most important British naval station here in the Carib Sea, and she needed to speak with the commanding officer here, that would be Admiral Cochrane. Would she be allowed to do so? The commander of a large naval station like this would have many demands on his time.

Jater interrupted her reverie. 'Our guard ship, our prize, at the dock. Do we get our money?'

Corrie raised her voice so that her crew could hear her reply. 'The prize court will have looked the guard ship over by now, Yeoman. That will mean money in all of our pockets.'

One quarter of the value of a prize would be divided among the hands. Corrie herself would receive a quarter, or maybe even half the value of the guard ship, if Admiral Cochrane did not claim his share, but she was sure would claim his share. Admirals serving abroad relied heavily on prize money to make their personal fortunes.

Her crew gave a rousing cheer. They looked forward going ashore with money in their pockets.

Corrie made a silent resolve to prevent *any* of her people going ashore, lest they bring tropical fevers aboard.

'Signal from Clarence House, captain. COME ASHORE AND REPORT.'

'Very well. Signal my brother's ship the *Belle Poule*. MEET ME AT CLARENCE HOUSE.

'Mr. Potts, I'll want you to come with me. We may have to bully our way in. Better change into your Number Ones. Try to look impressive. This will be an official visit. Admiral Cochrane is second only to God. I shall need you at my side. Ask Norah to look after Nathaniel.'

Corrie hurried below to put on her best uniform.

Half an hour later, two smartly dressed marines sprang to attention as Corrie, her brother James and Lieutenant Potts climbed the broad steps to the pillared portico of Clarence House, an imposing building boasting no less than eight white columns. Clarence House was the admiral's place of work. The double doors were swung open for them by a pair of liveried doormen.

Indoors, Corrie took off her plumed hat and tucked the thing under her arm. Tom did the same with his own hat.

Her brother James whispered to his sister. 'The *Belle Poule* is seaworthy. Don't be fooled by her appearance.'

'I'll bear that in mind,' said Corrie.

In the main hall they encountered a supercilious aide-de-camp who looked them over with a practiced eye. 'You are...?' he rasped.

Corrie knew better than to answer.

Instead she nodded to Tom.

This was the ancient game of precedence.

The snotty-nosed aide had to figure out who was the more important of this newly-arrived trio and whether any of the three deserved to be admitted to the august and sacred presence of the naval station's admiral in command, who was, when all was said and done, the King's proxy, exerting godly powers. Corrie had no doubt whatsoever that every day a host of naval officers would show up here at Clarence House searching for appointments and begging for stores requisitions.

'Captain Sir Corrie Harriman, here at the request of Admiral Cochrane,' replied Tom. 'This is Captain James Harriman. I am Lieutenant Potts.'

'The nature of this request?' asked the aide cunningly. If there was any news that was of importance, here was a chance for this aide to shine in the admiral's eyes by being the first to bring him an important report.

'The matter is for the Admiral's ears only,' said Corrie curtly, dashing the aide's hopes.

'Time is of essence,' added Tom for good measure.

The aide was not impressed. So there was nothing in it for him? He'd see about *that*. 'That won't do, gentlemen,' the aide replied haughtily. 'The Admiral is a presently in conference in the Grand Salon with Admiral Wentworth and with Sir John Thomas Duckworth. If you come back tomorrow and can give me a plausible reason, you may be allowed to see him. The Admiral is a busy man.'

Corrie shook her head. 'If Admiral Wentworth is here, and talking to Duckworth and Cochrane, then all three of us must join the conference immediately. Go tell your boss Harriman is here with vital information about the French squadron. Be quick! There is no time to be lost. Move! That's an order! Why are you standing there gawping? We are at war with the French.'

The aide went red in the face. 'I have told you the Admiral is too busy to see you. I must ask all three of you to leave right now, or I shall have to summon the guard to have you thrown out of the building.'

'Enough is enough,' retorted Corrie angrily. 'Come along, Tom! Come on, James. We can find the Grand Salon by ourselves.'

'The Grand Salon,' said Tom, putting his face very close to that of the aide.

The aide's eyes darted to the left.

Tom shoved the aide to one side.

The three officers strode towards a door sculpted in bas relief with a rendering Neptune carrying a three-pronged trident on his shoulder.

Tom knocked and opened the door.

The strode into a high ceilinged chamber.

Three admirals were looking at a chart spread out before them on a handsome mahogany table. A fan operated by Islander revolved slowly overhead, wafting cool air about the salon.

Tom came to attention and announced in a loud voice 'Captain Sir Corrie Harriman, Knight Commander of the Most Honourable Order of the Bath. Captain James Harriman. Lieutenant Potts!'

Corrie's mother, Admiral Wentworth, who was one of the three admirals, spun on her heel. 'Corrie!' she exclaimed. 'How good to see you! What are you doing here in the Carib Sea? Allow me to introduce my fellow admirals. This is Admiral Cochrane, who runs this Leeward Islands station, and this is Sir John Thomas Duckworth, whose squadron you will have seen out in the harbour. My fellow admirals, may I introduce Captain Corrie Harriman who brought the China Fleet to London, served in the *Victory* at Trafalgar. This is her brother Captain James Harriman, captain in the *Belle Poule*, and, if I am not mistaken, her first lieutenant.'

Both Corrie and her mother Admiral Wentworth were both disguised as men, and dared not hug each other. Instead they shook hands.

Then Corrie strode straight to the chart. 'A day ago we had a brush with Leissègues here,' she said, tapping her finger on the chart. 'Leissègues is transporting a thousand soldiers to Santo Domingo to reinforce the garrison there. The French ships have storm damage and some battle damage. When last seen, Leissègues was proceeding westwards along this coast. We have a favourable wind. We have a chance to sink the French before they disembark their troops. What is your readiness, Sir Thomas?'

Admiral Duckworth looked searchingly at Corrie. 'How did you find out how many soldiers they are transporting?'

'My brother and I boarded the enemy flagship. My brother can verify the number.'

'At least a thousand,' said James. 'Many of them Islanders. Armed with muskets.'

The three admirals exchanged meaningful glances.

'How soon can your squadron sail, admiral?' asked Corrie.

'We can sail today,' replied Duckworth. 'If the Commander of the Leeward Islands station thinks that advisable?'

Admiral Cochrane smiled. 'You all know that Lord Barham gave the order to relax the blockade of Brest?' he asked.

Corrie nodded.

Tom nodded.

James nodded.

Admiral Duckworth nodded.

Admiral Wentworth nodded.

Yes, they all knew what the First Lord had done.

Cochrane went on in measured tones: 'What you may not know, gentlemen, and I have this in confidence from the First Lord himself, is the reason *why* he relaxed the blockade.'

Corrie snapped her fingers. 'Trafalgar!' she said. 'Of course!' Barham was no idiot! On the contrary, he was a canny First Lord with plenty of experience in the Navy. Barham had known *exactly* what he was doing in ordering the lifting of the blockade.

Admiral Cochrane nodded.

Tom was not quite there yet. He was better at natural philosophy than politics.

Admiral Wentworth gazed at her daughter thoughtfully. So Corrie had acquired an edge. Perhaps the lack of news regarding her father had hardened Corrie's resolve, just as it hardened Admiral Wentworth's determination to make the French suffer. Perhaps at the bottom of their hearts both wife and daughter wanted Archibald's death to mean something, and they were anxious to bring this naval war to a quick and successful conclusion.

Admiral Cochrane said 'Yes, Lord Barham was of the opinion that the seas would never belong wholly to Britain until the French first-rates in Brest had left their safe haven and ventured forth into the Atlantic to be destroyed. We had word that Napoleon had been simply furious about being defeated at Trafalgar and wished to be. avenged immediately. They said the tyrant was anxious for his navy to win a major battle at sea in order to restore what he termed *the reputation of France as a naval power*. Between you and me, Napoleon's real anxiety is that the French slave plantations here in the Carib Sea, which provide him with valuable funds for his armies, might fall into our hands. So he decided to hit England *and her abolitionists* in the eye by sending this naval expedition under Leissègues to reinforce his possessions in this theatre of the war. He has ordered his ships to put ashore troops. By so doing he hopes to restore confidence in the naval prowess of France. As soon as Lord Barham heard of Napoleon's anger, he gave the order to lift the blockade of Brest. The idea was to *tempt* Napoleon's French first-rates to go to sea. The First Lord wrote me a letter ordering me to destroy the French warships should they turn up here in the Carib Sea, and now it seems they *have* come here, so I think we had better deal with them, gentlemen. To put it plainly, we must sink them. Here is our chance to demonstrate once and for all that it is we, the British, and *not* the French, who command the seas. Go get them, gentlemen!'

The five officers left Clarence House, brushing aside the purple-faced aide and a squad of marines summoned to the antechamber to arrest the three officers who had barged in on three admirals during an important conference.

On the steps of Clarence House, Corrie and her mother paused for a moment for a quick and very private exchange.

'When did you last see him?' her mother asked her daughter.

Corrie regarded her mother steadfastly as she replied 'It was my fault. I ordered him aboard a captured enemy vessel to act as prizemaster at the height of the battle off Cape Trafalgar. I have not seen him since. You have had no word from the Admiralty?'

Her mother shook her head. 'Sir Erasmus Gower, the new Commanding Officer of the St. John's Naval Station, thinks that Archibald may be among the wounded.'

Corrie nodded. 'It is just possible, I suppose. It was hard to account for all those missing from the *Victory* after the fighting was halted. It was a truly terrible battle. We may have to manage without him. I miss him! In our family play about Puss-in-Boots, I laughed so much that I forgot my lines.'

Her mother nodded. 'I miss him, too. I hope you and Tom are making the most of the time you have together?'

'I think so. Tom?'

Tom nodded. 'We are.'

Corrie's mother made an effort and pulled herself together. 'I think this is when we shake hands and rejoin our three ships. I believe Cochrane is right in saying that if we sink this French squadron led by Admiral Leissègues, we shall win the seas for Britain.'

'Good luck to us all,' ventured Tom, who had known for years that the Admiral Wentworth was Corrie's mother.

Corrie remembered how her father nearly died on that horrible island of Cabrera, but had won through in the end. Her father had been so thin and pale at the end of that ordeal.

She was going to miss him dreadfully now that he was gone for good.

16

CHAPTER

THE TROPICAL STORM HAD RETURNED.

Corrie watched the fronds of the palm trees on the coast of Santo Domingo thrash about madly as if in a fit of convulsion. The French would be unwise to try disembarking their troops in a wind like this, but she could see the French flagship sailing close inshore.

'Signal the *Belle Poule*. ENGAGE THE ENEMY. Mr. Potts, make ready our bow-chaser.'

'Aye aye, sir,' said Tom. 'Chain-shot?'

Corrie nodded. Chain-shot might damage the French rigging.

Jeanette sponged out the barrel of the nine-pounder..

Fraser loaded the piece.

Jeanette saw to the priming, and gave Fraser a nod. She was ready to fire the weapon.

Billy sang out from the masthead. 'Sails beyond headland, captain! Tun up! Wicked! One of dem she is *Invulnerable*!'

Corrie spun on her heel and grabbed a telescope from her time-keeper.

Her mother's flagship? Here?

There was no mistaking that set of sails. Her mother's flagship was accompanied by a frigate. So here was their chance to teach Contre-Amiral Corentin Urbain de Leissègues that Trafalgar had been no accident. But in this wind her spanking new galley would be useless.

How would the French admiral react? Leissègues was a strategist. His first command had been the brig *Furet*, off Newfoundland. He was a man of feeling. He had freed 22 slaves. Was that jaundiced Captain Bigot with him?

Lightning lit up the clouds.

Thunder rumbled.

The enemy had formed a line of battle. There was the *Alexandre* in the lead, as clear as day. The French squadron was heading up the coast towards Nizao. They had their smaller vessels tucked away between their line of battle and the shore.

Corrie sucked in her breath. Something had changed quite suddenly. The air smelled different.

She looked in disbelief at the palm trees. She was not dreaming. The fronds had ceased the gyrations! The agitated seas, so rough only a few minutes ago, had become as calm and still as a millpond. This was uncanny. This was unprecedented. She threw a questioning look at her ageing sailing master, Mr. Weevil.

Weevil touched his forehand to his cap as he had been taught to do when addressing his captain. 'The Eye of the Storm,' he said.

The Eye of the Storm!

Of course!

Corrie suddenly recalled her governess Mrs. Demeter reading from Herodotus, who had nothing but praise for the triremes, the double-banked warships of ancient days propelled by oars and provided with sharp prows with which to slice enemy vessels in half. If Herodotus was to be believed, the Battle of Salamis against the massive fleet of Xerxes had been defeated in a naval battle *fought in a dead calm just like this*, and defeated by *galleys*. Corrie bit her lip.

Her galley! Of course! The French don't know about my galley. They don't know I can attack them in this windless calm.

Here was the chance of a lifetime. Here was an opportunity to launch her galley and free the entire naval world from the predations of the French.

Here I come, Napoleon! I have felt you breathing down my neck all my life. Today I shall breathe down your neck. Off Cape Trafalgar I saw Nelson break the French line. Today I shall break the French line again. What an opportunity! I shall attack at once.

'Launch the galley! All those who attacked the French guard ship in the mouth of the Gironde, arm yourselves and man the galley. Lie flat in the bottom of the galley just as you did before. Surprise is everything. Mr. Potts, the ship is yours. I'm going in the galley.'

Tom's jar dropped. He shook his head. 'You can't lead the attack *yourself*,' he protested. 'You're the captain. You have to stay with the *Swift*.'

Corrie lowered her voice. 'Not this time, Tom. This one is mine. Look after Nathaniel. If I don't come back, tell him I loved him.'

Corrie leaped into the stern of the galley and grabbed the tiller. All her people had clambered aboard. 'Cast off! Make way! This is our chance to win the war. Row for your lives, people!' Corrie began to slam the galley's side with her palm to give the rowers their time.

'Sing!' shouted Corrie.

'Who'll drag a *buckie*?' sang John Eaves.

'I'll drag a *clam*,' growled the women and men at the oars.

'I'll drag a *buckie*,' sang Corrie. 'And I'll be *lucky*. And I'll be no *lang*.'

The singing of the shanty helped the rowers keep time as they drove the galley faster and faster through the clear, still tropical water. Looking over the side, Corrie could see the long dark shadow of her galley passing across bright purple and crimson corals, scattering hundreds of bright blue and yellow fishes.

She increased the tempo as they sped towards the gaping hole in the stern of the French flagship.

In their previous encounter with the *Impérial* her gun crews had pounded the stern of the enemy flagship, smashing in the windows of the French admiral's Great Cabin. Today she would use those gaping holes to swarm aboard and take the French by surprise. She had learned in her previous attack on the battleship that the *Impérial* was *crammed with French soldiers* destined for the French garrison. Those soldiers would be armed with muskets. This was not going to be easy.

The odds were against them.

At least she had the element of surprise. She had her hundred women and men hidden in the bottom boards of this galley, spoiling for a fight. The French deserved to be taught a lesson, and, by George, her people were going to avenge those half-drowned enemy bandsmen.

Corrie knew her people. She knew what made them hopping mad. Here was their chance to teach the French to behave like civilized human beings. Her crew thought they had the high moral ground, bless them!

Quicker and quicker she beat the side of her galley, and faster and faster her galley flew through the clear still water, closing rapidly with the French flagship's vulnerable stern.

She chose her moment.

'Oars!'

The rowers held their eighteen oars high and vertical like a forest of young trees. Corrie leaned on the tiller and brought her lovely galley swinging around until she lodged herself firmly among the smashed frames of the French admiral's ruined cabin.

'Board!' she cried, and leapt for the enemy ship.

Her people tumbled after her, brandishing their weapons.

They found the *Impérial*'s Great Cabin empty. There was nobody there to fend off their attack. Where had all those enemy soldiers gone? Had that mad Captain Bigot ordered them all drowned?

Filled with growing misgivings, Corrie dashed up the companionway steps.

She burst onto the enemy Quarter Deck.

She was just in time to see the last of the French soldiers run up the white coral sand beach and vanish into the thick forest. Damn! Apparently the *Impérial*'s boats had carried them ashore, taking advantage of the Eye of the Storm.

Leisségues doffed his hat politely. 'I have disembarked our troops and fulfilled my mission for my Emperor. A pleasure to meet you again, Sir Corrie.'

She and Leisségues had met briefly during the brief Peace that had preceded the resumption of the war. She did respect Leisségues. He was a formidable adversary.

Corrie replied by stating her own opinion of the French Admiral's hurried landing of soldiers. 'It is a hundred miles to the garrison. Your troops will wade through swamps. They will succumb to Yellow Fever, Dengue and Malaria. What has become of your Captain Bigot?'

Leisségues nodded. 'He too has run off into the forest. I think the poor fellow has lost his mind. But what are your plans for me? You have me at a disadvantage. Most of my people are still ashore handling the disembarkation. I don't know how you managed to attack me in this dead calm but I sense a change in the weather. I fear the Eye of the Cyclone will soon be passing.'

'Yes,' replied Corrie, glancing up at the sky. 'Already the wind is veering and strengthening. I hope you will forgive me for the order I must now give.'

Her boarding party had followed her instructions and seized command of the enemy's Quarter Deck.

'Jensen, the wheel. Hard to starboard. Steer this enemy flagship onto the reef.'

'Aye, captain,' said the Dane phlegmatically. 'Hard to starboard, it is. Better hang on to something, captain. She's about to hit hard.'

Admiral Leisségues closed his eyes.

'Everybody grab at stays and ringbolts and brace themselves,' ordered Corrie.

Somewhere among the palm trees Captain Bigot gave a cry of anguish. 'NO!' he shouted, struggling ineffectively to escape from the strong arms of an Islander.

'Here it come,' said Jensen, and closed his eyes.

The French flagship hit the reef with an almighty crunch of breaking timber. The masts broke off. The rigging tumbled down. They were less than a mile from the beach.

Admiral Leisségues shouted '*Sauve qui peut!*

'Back to our galley, you Swifts!' cried Corrie. 'Our work is done here.'

Obeying her order with alacrity, her men and women let go of their French prisoners, dodged through the fallen shrouds, jumped over the tumbled blocks and smashed yards of the ruined French flagship, and then tumbled down to lie flat in their long narrow craft with efficiency acquired during many long drills.

Then the eighteen oarsmen took up their positions and looked to Corrie for orders.

'Cast off and pull for the *Swift!*'

Her people did as she bid.

They sent their galley racing back to their own frigate. They were in a hurry. The weather was changing by the minute.

Corrie was the first to leap back aboard the *Swift*.

She ran to the binnacle and stared about her wildly. How was the battle going? How were the ships of Duckworth's squadron faring?

The *Diomède* had swung out of line to follow the unexpected shoreward turn of the *Impérial*. Both the French 74 and the French flagship were fast on the same reef with their masts and rigging hopelessly tumbled about their decks. Neither were salvable.

Captain Garreau of the French 80-gun *Alexandre* had used the sudden change in the direction of the hurricane to surprise the British by deftly inserted his warship into the gap between two British vessels: the *Spencer* and the *Northumberland*. Corrie watched grimly as the French captain opened fire with both his port and starboard batteries, raking both British vessels. Corrie could hear the cries of wounded women, children and men. She heard officers yell desperate orders.

She turned on her heel.

Several British frigates had following Corrie's example and made prizes of the French.

They were setting fire to French vessels deemed beyond saving.

Corrie closed her telescope with a snap. This was a substantial victory for the Royal Navy, following close on the heels of that resounding victory off Cape Trafalgar. The defeat of the French would celebrated in British possessions throughout the Carib Sea. Britain had put paid to Napoleon's last remaining hope of naval dominance, and Corrie's beautiful eighteen-oar galley of elm and ash built for her in Deal had saved the day for England.

'Private signal from the *Invulnerable*, captain. JOIN ME IN MY CARRIAGE.'

'Reply HEADING FOR CARABAS and take station on the *Invulnerable*, Jensen.'

'Aye aye, cap'n.'

Corrie exhaled. Time to head for home. She had an after-thought. 'Signal the *Invulnerable* again. WHAT OF PARTRIDGE AND ALLEN?'

A lengthy reply to this inquiry arrived by pigeon an hour later. Apparently the Quaker natural philosopher William Allen had visited the local British sugar plantation and documented the slavery there. Judging by what Corrie had gleaned from talking to her Captain of the Maintop, Billy Brown, who herself had escaped from a British sugar plantation, the visit would have left Allen gasping. She was sure Allen would continue to refuse to eat sugar for the rest of his life.

Meanwhile, Allen and Partridge were ordered to sail the guard ship back to London to convey the news of the victory to the Admiralty.

So she had lost her new officer, the hesitant Mr. Partridge, and might never see the earnest Mr. Allen again. Such were the fortunes of the Navy.

Corrie exhaled.

It was all over!

The French had been defeated. She and her mother were victorious and homeward bound. If only her father had not gone missing during the battle off Cape Trafalgar! In all probability neither she nor her mother would ever see Archibald again. That, too, was the way of the Navy. There were many, many friends and fellow officers Corrie would never see again. It unfortunate that her father should be one of them. She was on her way home. Her family home on the hill overlooking the harbour would not be the same without their father there to make them all laugh with his plays about cats wearing boots.

17

CHAPTER

CORRIE'S FATHER, LIEUTENANT ARCHIBALD HARRIMAN, was studying the captain's precious chart as the fishing schooner *Marie Spindler* rose and fell with swell after swell. He marked their noon position carefully with a cross, and then returned the captain's sextant to the velvet nest inside its handsome mahogany case.

Archibald stared at the trail of crosses wending its way across the vast expanse of the Atlantic Ocean. This had been a very bad time of year to cross the Atlantic. The trade winds had been East North East and North, and they had been bitterly cold.

The skipper of the *Marie Spindler* had injured himself a few days earlier while making burnt ocky for the boy. The skipper was laid out in his bunk sucking at a sliver of raw fish for a remedy.

During the crossing, three of the schooner's hands had suffered back injuries hauling nets, but all three were tough, strong men, and were recovering fast.

Thank God the *Marie Spindler* had escaped from Gibraltar without incurring the wrath of the Navy. He had fooled that guard boat. Not bad for a Green Man!

About midway through the voyage, their schooner had fought her way through two big storms that might easily have committed all their bodies to the deep, to be turned into corruption, looking for resurrection when the Sea gave up her dead, and in the promise of a life to come.

Archibald had nursed his healing leg. The limb was mending well. For that he gave silent thanks.

The ship's boy Tommy had survived both storms, and today was in his hammock, wrapped in a blanket, telling stories to his mouse and munging on a piece of oaten cake.

Archibald was confident that none of the crew were contagious. The voyage had lasted a full five weeks. There had been no signs of miasmic contagion among the women and men.

The merry-begot ownshook of a First Mate, Johnny Magorey, tossed back a callibogus of spruce beer and the rum.

'Where are we today?' he asked, peering over Archibald's shoulder.

'About here,' Archibald replied. Pointing to his most recent X.

'Within hailing distance of St. John's! Not bad for a by-boat.'

Archibald nodded. 'We may sight the Narrows very soon, if I haven't made a mistake.'

The Mate took another swig. 'No mistake. I hear the bauks calling. How's our skipper today?'

Archibald lowered his voice. 'Still in pain.'

'So I'm the principal man, then, for bringing us into harbour?'

'You are indeed, Mr. Magorey. And an extra ten pounds for yourself if you sell our haul of fish to Nobles.'

'Aye. Then I had better stir my stumps and earn that ten pounds,' replied Magorey.

Archibald nodded. 'Need help?'

Magorey shook his head.

'Call if you need me,' said Archibald and went aft to feed a chunk of wood into the fire in the ship's galley. He stirred the embers with a poker.

The crew's thick woolen socks, washed in salt water, were pegged out on a line to dry over the iron stove. They were pungent. Nauseating, to be truthful. His wounded leg be damned, he would rather be out on deck than cooped up down here below deck.

'What happens when you die?' asked the ship's boy out of nowhere, looking up at him from his hammock.

Archibald looked the lad in the eye. 'Nobody knows, Tommy. Nobody has come back from the dead to tell us.'

'Am I going to die?'

That was a serious question that deserved a serious answer.

'Not today. One day, yes, you will die. Everybody dies sooner or later. Even that flat-faced mouse of yours will die. Did you find that mouse hiding in a tunnel under some long grass?'

The boy's jaw dropped. 'How did you know?'

'He's a meadow vole. That's where meadow voles live. In their tunnels under the grass. What's the mouse's name?'

'Mouses don't have names. Do they?'

'*Mice* don't have names, no, but you may give your mouse a name. What would be a good name for him?'

The boy scratched his head. 'He likes running about. How about Speedy?'

'Speedy is good name for a mouse. You may take Speedy up on deck to see the view as we sail into the Narrows.'

'Are we really *arriving*? Are you *sure*?'

'Unless I have miscalculated, we are entering St. John's Harbour. I can hear the cries of the eagles.'

'Do eagles eat mice?'

'They prefer fish or squirrels.'

'Come on Speedy! Let's go see the eagles.'

The lad darted up on deck.

Archibald followed the youngster up the steps.

Yes, they were sliding through the Narrows into the natural harbour surrounded by hills that were most familiar to him. An eagle flew by overhead. A dugong barked.

The naval base had changed somewhat in the years since the beginning of the war. Newcomers, many from Ireland, now crowded the Upper Path and the Lower Path. The demand for salt fish was growing. The price of fish was rising. The skipper of the *Marie Spindler* would do well out of this voyage, providing he did not breathe a word about the manner of his escape from Gibraltar. Archibald stared at all the new storehouses and alehouses crowding the north side of the harbour, and was amazed.

Was his wife still playing the part of Admiral Wentworth? There were fewer warships here in these sheltered waters than he had expected. Where was the navy? Were they out patrolling the Grand Banks? He saw no sign at all of his wife's flagship, the *Invulnerable.* His heart beat faster. He had been away for ten years. He was not sure what to expect. Was his wife here? Or was she off having an adventure? Was he about to find their home abandoned, their hearth cold and their garden overgrown? Had his wife died? That was one grim possibility.

He ducked back down below to say goodbye to Captain Chaffey. 'Your Green Man thanks you captain. By your leave, I'll be going ashore now.'

'You have brought us straight to St. John's. I wish I had your skill with chart and sextant. I thank you, Lieutenant. I thank you for spiriting us out of Gibraltar. You have kept your side of our bargain.'

'And you have kept yours, skipper Chaffey.' He lowered his voice. 'I beg you to say nothing of our escape from Gibraltar. Don't breathe a word about slipping past that guard boat under cover of darkness. We could all be hanged.'

'I'm no scumshy.'

'Good fortune to you, then! May you sell your catch!'

'Will you be wanting a share?'

Archibald shook his head. 'Not for myself. You'll be giving the lad something?'

Chaffey nodded. 'I shall.'

'Then I'm content.'

They shook hands.

The *Marie Spindler* found her berth.

Archibald shook hands with the men, said goodbye to the Tommy and Speedy, and jumped ashore.

It was strange being back on land. The ground seemed to heave and then drop away as if he were still at sea, which was only to be expected, but a little difficult to manage with his gammy leg.

He limped along the Lower Path. Evidently the war had brought new prosperity to the fishery. Everywhere he looked he spied new warehouses and ship chandlers selling oil, paint, clams and glassen bobbers.

He took a short cut to the Upper Path, and then headed toward the naval base. He was not ready to report in. First he was anxious to see if his wife was still alive and his home in one piece.

Like Odysseus returning home from the Trojan War, he had no way of knowing what to expect after having been away for ten years. Would he have to disguise himself as a beggar and slay her suitors?

He entered the orchard where his children had spent long hours playing at naval battles and bunging apples at each other. The branches were bare and scary this early in the year. Here was his two-and-a-half-storey wooden hip-roofed house with the familiar central chimney. It was good to know the house still stood. That was a relief.

He saw a puff of blue wood-smoke emerge from the chimney only to be blown away by the breeze.

Someone was at home.

He quickened his pace.

He staggered up the garden path.

Nobody locked their doors in St. John's. The penalty for theft was hanging.

Very carefully he eased open the front door of Harriman House, making sure the brass dolphin knocker did not make a sound to announce his arrival. It would be fun to surprise his wife. He tip-toed into the hall, shrugged off his coat and hung the garment on the familiar coat rack he and his wife had erected near the umbrella stand. He heard a noise in the parlour. He heard the clatter of tongs and poker. Was this wife stoking the fire? Was he about to surprise her?

He entered the room.

It was *not* his wife.

His heart sank.

But who was it?

Who was this woman behaving as if she owned the place?

It took him a moment to recall that this lady wiping her hands on her apron was none other than his children's governess, the long-ago widowed Mrs. Demeter.

Mrs. Demeter turned and saw him. Her jaw dropped. Her eyes grew as big as saucers as if she were seeing a ghost. 'Lieutenant Harriman? How wonderful to see you again, sir! Why, we thought you were dead. There was no word of your whereabouts after that big battle…'

'My wife?' asked Archibald, impatiently.

'Oh, she's gone. Sir. I'm sorry. She left the day after she was replaced as Governor by Sir Erasmus Gower. She sailed in the *Invulnerable*. She said something about being off to deal with a French squadron? I believe she had another ship for company. I forget which one. Sir, about the children…'

Archibald bit his lip. 'James and Corrie?' he asked, bracing himself. 'Are they all right?'

'What I was going to say, sir, was that I never meant for them to go to sea so young. When I made those costumes for them I thought they were going to act out one of your family plays like Riquet-with-the-Tuft and Little Red Riding Hood. I knew Corrie was mad about Perrault. I was so proud of her, reading in French at her young age. Can you imagine? And she was a good influence on her brother James who I declare never read a book in his life save those I made him read. In fact we were in the middle of Book Twelve of the Odyssey. I expect you know the passage. *Hearts of oak, did you go down alive into the homes of Death? Sailing directions, landmarks, perils…* Well, I was sure James and Corrie would be back for more, and then the next morning they had simply gone.

They never came home. I wept for them. I had myself rowed out to remonstrate with Captain Redburn, but the *Swift* sailed while I was still on my way out to the ship. Both your lovely children snatched away to serve in the Navy. It was too much to bear. I mean James I could understand, but Corrie? My heart leapt into my mouth! What would happen to Corrie trapped in the belly of a warship? She had dressed herself up as a young man. I wondered what would happen to her when they found out she was a woman? I tell you, Lieutenant Harriman, the bottom fell out of my world that day they were snatched away by the Press Gang!'

Archibald did his best to contain his impatience. 'Mrs. Demeter! I know what happened to James and Corrie six years ago. You were not to blame. But what I am asking you for today is news of James and Corrie today. Are they alive? Did they survive Trafalgar?

Mrs. Demeter stared at him. 'Oh, my God! You didn't know? Nobody told you?'

Archibald froze. 'Nobody told me *what*, Mrs. Demeter? You try my patience.'

'Corrie was knighted. She's Sir Corrie now. And both she and James, you won't believe this, they are both are in command of their own frigates. Corrie is in command of the very frigate she was hauled aboard by that dreadful Press Gang on that moonlit night when they went down to the Crown and Anchor to dance their hornpipe. Now she is commander of the *Swift*. Your wife says that James has a frigate, too. His is called *La Belle Poule*.'

'Mrs. Demeter. There is a war going on. I'll try to make this very simple. Is my wife alive?'

'Yes.'

'Are my children alive?'

'Last I heard.'

Archibald limped to the rocking chair by the fire. He collapsed into it. He was drained. 'Thank you, Mrs. Demeter,' he said flatly.

Mrs. Demeter stared at him. 'You've hurt your leg? I'll make you a cup of tea. When did you eat last?'

'I don't remember. Where are my family? Why are they not here?'

'I can't answer for James or Corrie, but as I said your wife sailed a month ago. Our new Governor, Sir Erasmus Gower, would have the latest news. Or you could try your wife's pigeon handler, Winifred. Winifred tells me she has been kept very busy this last week. While Winifred is not permitted to tell me any details, she did say there had been another battle.'

'Another battle?' blurted out Archibald, struggling back up onto his feet, cursing his crooked leg. 'Why the devil didn't you tell me that to begin with?'

Mrs. Demeter frowned. 'You are a naval officer. I thought you'd know all about battles and things like that.'

'I'm sorry. Of course. My mistake,' he said and then sank back into the comfort of his own rocking chair in his own home. After a while, he sighed and put his hands to the warmth of the fire. No news was better than bad news, he supposed. 'I'm a naval officer *missing in action* and *supposed to be dead*, Mrs. Demeter. Do me a kindness. Bring me that cup of tea and then be off with you to find your friend of yours who looks after the pigeons. Tell here I want to know who won the battle, and I don't want to ask the new Governor. And Mrs. Demeter, I don't blame you in the slightest for letting James and Corrie run away to join the navy six years ago. I am proud of them both, and I'm glad you taught them their Homer.

On hearing these words, Mrs. Demeter's face broke out in a wonderful smile. For long she had lived with guilt of letting her charges escape and here at last was their father returned from the war to say she was not to blame after all! She went to fill the kettle with a lighter heart.

By the time she returned, the Lieutenant had fallen asleep seated in his chair by his own hearth. Very gently she placed the teapot, mug and milk and sugar on the side table, together with a vanilla custard pudding and a bowl of blueberries. Then she tiptoed out of the house and went in search of the pigeon handler.

A thick white mist hid from her view the four battered warships that were feeling their way in through the Narrows to find a safe anchor in the Inner Harbour.

18

CHAPTER

CORRIE went ashore with Tom, Nathaniel, Ramón and Corrie's brother James and Corrie's mother Admiral Wentworth. Together they climbed the familiar hill path that led up to the naval station where a report would have to be made to Sir Erasmus.

Tom trailed behind. He had Nathaniel seated on his shoulders, and the lad Ramón for company. Tom had invited the Spanish lad to join them in this venture ashore, knowing that Ramón had no relatives in this part of the world. Nathaniel was interested in Ramón. From his high perch on his father's shoulders Nathaniel looked down on the boy from Spain as the boy this way and that, exploring the strange landscape of Newfoundland. He watched Ramón throw handfuls of half-melted snow into the air. He watched Ramón point in amazement at a bunch of bright crocuses bursting up out of the thawing beds of a private garden. Nathaniel decided that he would like to run about too. It seemed only fair to Nathaniel that if Ramon was allowed to run about and find crocuses, then he, Nathaniel, should be allowed to do so too. At a loss for words to explain this sudden need to join Ramón, Nathaniel twisted his body about to let his father know that he wanted to be put down.

When his father lowered him to the ground, Nathaniel suffered a big surprise. He had to struggle with the alarming novelty of being on solid land that did *not* heave up and down like the deck of a ship. Nathaniel complained loudly about this unmoving 'deck', so Tom hoiked his young son back up onto his ample shoulders.

Tom would not have to make a report to the Governor of the Naval Station. He was too junior in rank to do that. But he was delighted to be coming ashore with Corrie, and was hoping to be allowed to visit her family home. Here was a chance to compare her parents' establishment with that of his own father in England. He had often wondered what life had been like for Corrie growing up in a far-flung territory.

It was a shame they had lost brave Philip Broke, the captain of the *Shannon*, who had been killed during their engagement with the French flagship *Impérial*. The poor fellow had been cut in two by a French cannonade, and the young officer who had succeeded Broke as commander of the *Shannon* had been far too shy for such lofty company.

On the way up the hill from the dockside to the Governor's house, Corrie noticed a stream of smoke coming from the chimney of her childhood home. She threw her mother a questioning glance.

'Your governess Mrs. Demeter,' Admiral Wentworth replied shortly. 'I asked her to keep an eye on the house in my absence,' she added, quelling any hopes Corrie might have had regarding her missing father.

But at the mention of Mrs. Demeter, Corrie and James exchanged looks, recalling long hours spent together as children construing Homer in the summerhouse under Mrs. Demeter's watchful eye! Their governess was still alive! Perhaps they would have a chance to apologize to Mrs. Demeter for running away to sea on that moonlit night six years ago. It was strange to think how those six years had transformed the pair into able naval officers.

Sir Erasmus welcomed the three officers to his office while Tom and the children amused themselves on the parade ground, where some Navy children from the Barracks were playing Tiddly, a curious Newfoundland game that involved sticks, stones, and a great deal of running about and shouting.

The Governor listened carefully to their reports. He then expressed himself delighted by their success, and straightway ordered guns fired in celebration of the victory. He ordered his Marine Band to parade along the Upper and Lower Paths playing 'Heart of Oak' to spread the news of the defeat of Napoleon's squadron throughout the local populace, which these days numbered nearly eight thousand souls.

After they took their leave of the Governor, the three picked up Tom and the two boys, and headed down the hill to Harriman House.

If only my father were here to enjoy our triumph, Corrie thought. Listening to the band playing in the distance. She would never see her father again. She wiped a tear from her eye surreptitiously, hoping that her mother would not notice.

'He's dead,' Corrie said to herself quietly, facing up at long last to the reality of her father's demise. Her father was not going to be there for her anymore. No more Archibald. No more laughter and Puss-in-Boots.

Of course her mother noticed her tear.

As they made their way back down the hill to rejoin their ships, with Tom and the boys in tow, her mother turned to her grown-up children and asked 'Shall we drop by our house and have a word with Mrs. Demeter? Your governess will be delighted to hear the news, and pleased to see you both back home safe and sound.'

'Yes,' said Corrie, pulling herself together. 'Mrs. Demeter. Of course. Why not?'

James nodded. 'Good to see the old bird again.'

So they walked through the orchard and up to their family home.

They came to that familiar front door with its brass dolphin knocker.

Nathaniel begged to be allowed to touch the shiny dolphin to discover what it felt like.

Ramón was invited to bang the dolphin's tail on the door.

Bang! Bang! Bang! went the dolphin.

They heard footsteps inside the house.

Somebody was coming to answer the door.

Somebody with a limp.

The door opened.

It was Corrie's father.

Admiral Wentworth's jaw dropped.

'Archibald?' she whispered, unbelieving, and then opened her arms wide to welcome her husband back home after ten long years fighting in the war.

Archibald took her in his arms. He had long awaited this moment.

It was the end of his Odyssey.

Now from his breast into the eyes the ache
of longing mounted, and he wept at last,
his dear wife, clear and faithful, in his arms.

How the French Were Defeated

Photograph by Lance Croutear

Thank you so much for reading HOMEWARD BOUND! Naval historians have concluded that the defeat of Admiral Leissègues' squadron in the Battle of San Domingo put an end to Napoleon's ambition to have France become a naval power to rival the Royal Navy of Great Britain. But how exactly were the French defeated? When the Impérial engaged both leading British ships, and the Northumberland intervened to try to save the British flagship, we are told the French bombardment became so heavy that shot passed straight through both sides of the Northumberland and damaged the Superb, yet no account of the battle that I have read has explained to my satisfaction why the French flagship suddenly veered off course and then ran aground on a coral reef less than a mile from the beach.

Surely Corrie was responsible. Corrie steered the French flagship onto the reef. The Admiralty, having become aware that Corrie was a woman dressed in male attire, would not have dared to credit her with playing this important part in the engagement. Women were not supposed to serve in the Navy. That women did serve, and served in considerable numbers, is made plain by a published letter from an irate admiral of the period complaining bitterly that the forty women on board his ship had wasted valuable drinking water washing clothes.

OTHER BOOKS IN THE SERIES

Here is a list of twenty novels that tell Corrie's story from the beginning:

Corrie's War: Book 1: Press Gang!

Corrie's War: Book 2: Enemy ship!

Corrie's War: Book 3: Clear for Action!

Corrie's War: Book 4: Under Fire!

Corrie's War: Book 5: Sea Rescue!

Corrie's War: Book 6: Storm Fury!

Corrie's War: Book 7: Danger on Land!

Corrie's War: Book 8: Surprise Attack!

Corrie's War: Book 9: Night Raid!

Corrie's War: Book 10: Battle Stations!

Corrie's War: Book 11: Storm the Fort!

Corrie's War: Book 12: Court Martial!

Corrie's War: Book 13: Water Spout!

Corrie's War: Book 14: Attack the Enemy!

Corrie's War: Book 15: Stand and Deliver!

Corrie's War: Book 16: Glory and Fury!

Corrie's War: Book 17: Steal the Victory!

Corrie's War: Book 18: England Expects!

Corrie's War: Book 19: Trafalgar!

Corrie's War: Book 20: Homeward Bound!

My sincere thanks to Lance Croutear for allowing me to publish two of his excellent photographs in this edition of *Homeward Bound!* In Corrie's day, the *Victory* was an example of the very latest naval technology. Built and refitted at Chatham Dockyard, she has survived to the present day, and is open to visitors in her dry dock at Portsmouth.